THIS MODERN MAN IS BEAT

Fawzy Zablah

THIS MODERN MAN IS BEAT

SIMI PRESS

ISBN 978-1-955585-03-3

Some of these stories appeared, in somewhat different form, in *Expat Press, Hobart. Acentos Review*, and *The Open End Blog*.

Opening quote published in *The Review of Contemporary Fiction*, vol 13.1, Spring 1993.

Cover art by Rafal Kucharczuk
Book design by Euan Monaghan

Simi Press
www.simipress.com

For my mother Gladys Bigit

IS: "You have lived more than seventy years of your
life in the United States. Do you still feel Iberian,
a citizen from Spain? Or are you now an American
like everybody else around here?"

FA: "Neither one nor the other. I guess I am a
frontier man that belongs to a world that is no more.
I am a traditionalist stubbornly loyal to what some
would think are outmoded principles."

—A conversation with Felipe Alfau by Ilan Stavans

Contents

All Our Italian Friends Are Dead

I was so broke I went to see my mother. She gave me money to pick up Chinese food.

There was a good place near my apartment called Jade Garden. I used to order all the time from there with my ex. I got egg foo young, sweet and sour chicken, pork fried rice, and three egg rolls. I filled up my plate twice. My mother really enjoyed the rice. We sat and talked about the old house we owned in El Salvador. The tenants were always late with the rent, and they finally paid. My Aunt Rosa and Uncle Freddy always collected the rent for us and sent it via Western Union. They were getting up there in age but still so in love it made me wonder if that was still possible.

"Your aunt is depressed. You should call her."

"Okay, I'll call her."

I hadn't talked to my aunt and uncle in months. Despite that, every time I called them, my aunt's sense of humor always remained after busting my chops of course. My uncle, who once studied agronomy, liked to talk about plants and fruits and when was the best time to pick the local green mango.

After eating, I went to the couch and called them. My uncle Freddy answered.

"Hello,"

"Uncle Freddy, it's me."

"Hey Habib! Long time no talk. How the heck are you?"

"I'm good, here at my mother's; just brought her lunch." I always felt the need to *emphasize* that I had not deserted my mother.

"That's good that you visit her! Don't let her get lonely."

"Of course, I'm fifteen minutes away, so I pass by often. How's Tía Rosi?"

"She hasn't been feeling too good. The osteoporosis is acting up. She also gets migraines every other day."

"What does the doctor say?"

"He said she's suffering from depression. That she needs to go out more. Stay busy. He gave her an anti-depressant, but she doesn't want to take it."

"You guys should go out to eat more. Maybe go get breakfast a couple of times a week?"

"Believe me Habib, I try to get her out of the house, but sometimes she wants to and then she changes her mind and we don't go anywhere. So what are you going to do?"

"I hear you. My mom is the same way sometimes."

"So how's everything with you? How's work?"

"Work is good. I just celebrated my 10th year anniversary with the company and things are great. Can't complain."

Actually, the job was turning my brain into mush, and I felt my life withering away like the spirit of a badly injured deer that had just been run over by an SUV on Alligator Alley. But I didn't tell him that.

"And what about the ladies? How are things in that department?"

"Things are good. There's a couple. You know, it's complicated."

I didn't *really* have a girlfriend. I had a female friend, who everybody thought I should date, but I didn't mention her because I didn't want to bring his hopes up with a white lie.

Currently, I was at the tail end of an intense love affair with a married woman that just discovered she was pregnant with a baby that could be mine, but I didn't bring that up either. So I pretended like I was just living a life of partying and casual sex with numerous women, which that wasn't even close to the truth either. I was 40, and in El Salvador my family was starting to think I was either gay or a weirdo.

"Are you still living at that apartment on the beach?"

"No, I moved to a place near my job. It's closer to mom too. Traffic was just so bad heading to work that I just got sick of driving."

"Traffic is bad everywhere now. Your aunt and I went to Santa Teclas the other day, and it took us like an hour. Santa Teclas is like two miles away. It's ridiculous. "

"Enrique took me to Santa Teclas when I visited last time. His girlfriend lived there. They took me to a restaurant where they gave you tapas with your alcohol. I had a really great time."

"Oh yeah, I know of a place like that. There was a place close to your grandmother's house, but it closed a few years ago."

"It was kind of like Spain, the tapas are free. They just charge you for the liquor."

"Oh, Spain. It's so beautiful. Have you been?"

"No, I saw it on TV. I have to go to Spain."

"You should go. Tell a buddy and go. You will love it. I have a cousin who went and they rented a car, went everywhere up and down the country and had a fabulous time."

"I've been to Rome. I was there for about five days in 2004."

"Oh, Italy is great too. I bet you ate well."

"Yes, the food was so good. So fresh. We mostly ate at this old lady's house across the street from the hostel. We didn't understand a word she said, but she fed us like if we were her kids. We were there in August and all the Romans had left for holiday. It was pretty desolate. My buddy gave me strict instructions to stay away from the Americans. He said, 'We're here to meet Italian girls, not Americans.'"

My uncle laughed a good hearty laugh that came through the receiver and out into my mother's living room.

"And what happened? Did you meet any Italian women?"

"I met this beautiful dark-haired girl at a dance club, where you pay the girls to dance Bachata with you. We danced the whole night, and I thought, I finally met the Italian woman of my dreams and then we started talking. Turns out she was Cuban."

A cacophony of laughter was all I heard. "That is so funny," he said, trying to speak mid laugh.

"Yeah, Rome was great. We did end up meeting some real Italians later. They're very good-looking people, and stylish like hell. I kept thinking I was in the middle of a GQ fashion shoot half the time. I made a couple of friends too that I still keep in touch with."

"Oh yes, they are lovely, your aunt and I had a lot of Italian friends here. They're all gone now. All of our Italian friends are dead."

"Really, all of them?"

"Yes, they're all dead. That's what happens when you get old; all your friends start passing away."

"Well, you guys need to make new friends."

*

"That's a very good point—younger ones that will outlive us."

After that, he passed the phone over to my aunt and I spoke with her for twenty minutes. I tried to tell her as many funny stories as possible. And she laughed like she used to laugh with me when I was a little kid. I could feel her spirit lifting as we talked more and more. It made me feel so good. I promised myself that I would call them more often.

The $5 calling card I was using to make the call made that muffled car horn noise that it was about to end, and as I tried to say goodbye, the call cut off.

I helped my mother wash the dishes, and took out the trash. I'd see her tomorrow, I said, for grocery shopping.

When I got back to my apartment complex, and as I parked my car, I looked up at my place on the third floor wishing the lights were on and she was waiting for me.

I climbed the three flights of stairs feeling fat and full from all the greasy Chinese food and entered my studio apartment out of breath. With my knees cracking, I turned on the lights, fed the cat, and hung up the laundry that I had left in the dryer. I stared at the wet bar. The rum she brought me from Puerto Rico was gone. The Canadian whiskey from when she went to see her brother in Montreal had just a quarter left. I finished both bottles mostly by myself. I think I was trying to drink her away, but by this late point in the game I was beginning to realize she was bottomless. So I ate half of a very potent marijuana edible and went to bed.

Oslo

Habib bin Habib Al-Fulan woke up one night shaking, disheveled, and spinning like a top because of a dream about chubby, black bombs falling over Miami. His heart beat so fast and his fear was so great that he made a decision, right then and there, to move to Norway. He knew a man that lived in Oslo.

That man's name was John Voorten. Habib met him while on vacation in New York City in December of 2001. They spoke for the first time in an empty sub shop as they sat across each other, one table away from each other, both hungry for friendship. What was said in the beginning is not important. John Voorten was staying at a hostel in Amsterdam Avenue with his sister. Habib was staying with a Dominican girl in Washington Heights. At that particular moment in both their lives, they were two boys lost in the city.

That night, they touched on many subjects, ranging from their own life goals to Eastern Philosophy. Later they moved their conversation to a Starbucks up the street where they tried to better explain their opinions about the world and everything in it.

By the middle of their discussion the subject took an abrupt turn to the nature of evil. Habib said that as far he was concerned, in the big picture, it didn't matter if a person was good or bad. The only thing that matters is conviction, he said. I don't think the universe cares about good or evil. Take Hitler for example. Here was a guy that was a nobody before 1913. No one had even heard of him because he was a failed artist—one of the noblest things a person can choose to be. But Hitler was successful in finding his calling, or what he was naturally talented at, which was rhetoric. That can be considered the first part of success. Then he became a man of action, which of course, is the second part of success.

John Voorten paid close attention to every word. To Habib, his new friend kind of looked like a rough, homeless blue-eyed Adonis with long, blond hair. He was also very tall and had large bony hands.

When Habib noticed that he was sounding like a philosophy major going over the same tired subjects that had been discussed for hundreds of years, he quickly changed the topic to music and watched John Voorten suddenly perk up.

I am a singer, John Voorten said, or at least, I aspire to have a singing career. My favorite singer is Billy Joel. John then went on an inspired rant about Billy Joel's music and career. He analyzed every album, and his best live shows. His excitement was so contagious that Habib thought about buying a Billy Joel CD when he got back to Florida.

John was going to stay in New York City for three more days, and they decided to spend them together exploring the city. During the day, they went to the MOMA or Museum of Natural History, and at night they hit the bars. For two of those nights, they ended the night at McSorley's Old Ale House in the East Village, chatting up the other tourists and the Irish bartenders like they were best friends with a long history together.

When their time together was up, Habib and his girlfriend escorted John and his sister to Grand Central Terminal. They were on their way to see a friend in Chicago, and then catch a flight to Norway after six months of travel.

And while riding on the 4 train, as they made their way to Grand Central Terminal, John Voorten smiled at Habib and without hesitating began to sing "New York State of Mind" in a capella. The subway car was empty, and John Voorten's voice rose and fell like a seagull in the open sea. It was a performance Habib would never forget.

When they said their goodbyes at the terminal, John Voorten told Habib that he was always welcome at his home in Norway. As time passed, they kept in touch via email and once even came close to meeting up when John returned to the States for a brief stopover.

Habib eventually emailed John about the dream with the bombs. Come to Oslo, John Voorten wrote back. I await you. I have a two-bedroom apartment and you can stay with me. I can help you find a job at my father's art gallery. You will love it here in my country of Norway.

With that, Habib was more confident about his decision. The only thing left for him to do now was to convince his family and friends to come to Oslo with him. He decided to start with his best friend Sebastian Montes. Sebastian was the one friend that was still not married with kids or living with a girlfriend. Sebastian was born in New York City but raised in Miami. His parents were from South America via Spain. Habib thought that he would be the easiest to convince because he was a traveler.

And one Thursday evening when they were lounging around Sebastian's apartment in Brickell drinking Merlot and smoking marijuana, Habib told Sebastian about his dream with the bombs.

What bombs? Sebastian asked. The bombs that are going to fall over Miami, the bombs from my dream, Habib said. I don't know about those bombs. I only know about the bombs in your face, Sebastian said, laughing. Habib smiled and took a toke of the joint. They drank and smoked more, and then Habib asked him if he would move to Oslo with him. I would rather go to Brazil, Sebastian said. I'd go to Oslo for vacation but not to live there. I'm going to Sao Paulo and get me a sweet, beautiful mulata.

As the early evening wore on, they decided to go bar hopping in Coconut Grove. They went to four bars. At the first bar, they had a pitcher of beer. They sipped their beer slowly, surrounded by UM kids who glowed the way all White people from up north glow and it made Habib think that he could never be as happy as those kids.

The second bar had a mechanical bull that was ridden mostly by girls as the guys cheered them on. There were lakes of blond girls in almost every corner, with pockets of male resistance in between. At that second bar, they shared a bison burger with goat cheese and had another pitcher of beer, followed by two rum and cokes. That was the place where they spent the most time, because they had been infatuated with a group of girls at the end of the bar whom they never bothered to approach.

The third bar was in the style of an English pub and that's where they met up with a friend who was working as manager. At that bar, they had two more rum and cokes and a shot of Jagger each. Habib also spent one dollar on the jukebox. He selected a Rage Against the Machine track. They talked about how the pub reminded them of their trip to Amsterdam the year before. It made them nostalgic and their spirits were up.

At the fourth bar they ran into a man that Sebastian had gotten drunk with on a previous occasion. The man had a shaved head and he was already drunk. Habib watched them have a 100-mph conversation in drunken speech only they could understand. In that bar, they each had a shot of tequila and a beer because that was the special. A shot and beer for $7.

At 1:30 a.m. the three of them decided to go to the man's condominium in Biscayne. The man needed a ride, telling Sebastian that he had some good cocaine and they could order a hooker on the way. Two birds with one stone baby, he said, beaming with liquid confidence. Two birds with one stone.

On the car ride to the condominium in Biscayne, the man sat in the back seat as Habib drove and Sebastian rode in the passenger seat. The man read the hooker ads in the free weekly out loud trying to get them pumped up.

When they got to the man's place, which was the penthouse suite, they wasted no time in snorting most of his cocaine and ordering prostitutes. They only ordered two girls because Habib wasn't interested in spending money.

But when the escorts arrived, their host said that he didn't have any money and started begging Sebastian to pay for him, saying things like he was "good for it" and "don't be an ass." Sebastian refused to give him any money and the escorts left. After that, their once gracious host got really angry and kicked them out. You snort my cocaine and you drink my drinks, the man said, and you can't let me borrow a little money—well get the fuck out!

And while driving back to Sebastian's apartment in Brickell, Habib was now in the mood for illegal sex and Oslo was on his mind. He thought about tricking Sebastian for an Oslo trip, pretending it would only be a vacation. Then after a week of being in Norway and seeing all the blond beauties he would decide to stay. And we'll continue to have our crazy adventures, thought Habib, but in Norway.

When they got to Sebastian's apartment, they called an escort service and decided on a pretty blond with a skinny body and big breasts. She was the girl with the biggest picture in the ad. Her name was Natalia.

As Habib tried to explain what they wanted to the person at the end of the line, he made sure to emphasize that they wanted the blond Natalia, the girl that was in the front of the ad. I want you to send me Natalia, Habib said, the blond girl in your ad. *Yes*, said the man on the phone, *of course, yes, Natalia, she's one of our most popular girls. We will send her to you, yes, the blond.* Does she exist? Habib asked. Does she exist? Sebastian repeated as he played with his fat orange cat on the black leather couch. *Excuse me?* Does she exist? Habib asked again, raising the tone of his voice. Is she real? *Yes*, said the man. Because I want the blond Natalia with the big boobs. Is she Norwegian? *No, she's from Pompano.* Send her to us, Habib said. *She will be at your address in 30 minutes or less.* Habib hung up the phone and the boys smiled.

After receiving a call from the escort's driver, they went downstairs to let the girl up. When the girl got out of the car, it was clear that she wasn't the one they had ordered. What stood in front of them was a brunette with an extremely curvaceous body in a short, black dress. When she smiled, the boys smiled.

Bait and switch, Habib said, making a fist. Bait and switch, repeated Sebastian, hopping up and down. Habib approached the driver and told him that this wasn't the girl they had ordered, that they had ordered Natalia, the girl from Pompano. Habib kept repeating that they wanted the blond from the ad, pointing out to the driver the photo in the ad. We want her, he said. The bait and switch ain't cool, Sebastian said, standing beside him. Where is the blond? Habib asked. *I understand,* the driver said. Do you? *Yes, you wanted Natalia, the blond girl. You don't like this one? She is Brazilian.* The boys looked at her. *I will have to call the office. It will take about forty-five minutes to an hour because she is with another client.*

The boys looked at each other and decided to take the girl the man had brought. *I will give you a discount,* the driver said, smiling. *Charge them only 140,* the driver told the girl.

They took the girl up to the apartment and Habib went first, because he wanted to go home soon as his father would be up waiting for him. For a second, while having sex with this beautiful Brazilian woman, Habib felt like he was in Rio De Janeiro, but he wanted to feel like he was entering a Norwegian goddess instead. The prostitute was very passionate and loving, and she laughed and said "oops" when Habib broke the condom inside her.

When they finished having sex, Habib put his clothes back on and thanked the girl for her services. He stood before her with his melancholy presence, trying not to be sad. She blew him a kiss that made his whole body shake. He came out to the living room with a smile. Sebastian smiled. You're up, Habib said. I'm calling it a night. See you later, said Sebastian as he ran into the bedroom and jumped in the bed.

While driving home, Habib was pulled over by a police officer by the name of Jose M. Fernandez. He failed the roadside test and he refused to take an alcohol blood level test. He was arrested and taken to the local police station to be processed. On the ride to the police station, while sitting in the back, Habib asked the police officer what the M in his name stood for, and the officer said Maria.

After being processed at the police station, Habib was taken by another officer to a prison, where his photo was taken and he was allowed one phone call. Habib called Sebastian because he didn't want to worry his father. Sebastian's cell went to voicemail and he left a message.

He was then put into a glass cell with eight other inmates. After about twenty minutes, all the inmates were shackled in twos and put in a gray, rusty bus and taken to another prison in downtown Miami where, ironically, his journey had begun.

Habib was shackled next to a short Hispanic kid who couldn't have been older than twenty-one.

As they rode in the bus, a horrible feeling came over him as if they were all being taken to a slaughterhouse. As he watched the sun rise above the earth in the very early morning, he tried to think about anything else but his own present situation, and when he thought about his father, an even greater fear engulfed him very much like the one from the dream about the bombs. And what about Oslo now? he thought to himself.

When the bus arrived at the prison, they were all led by armed guards to a big cell on the second floor that could hold about fifty men. Each couple was unshackled before entering the cell. Once inside, as new inmates, each one had to go and claim a bunk, but Habib sat at a picnic table by the front instead. He sat next to a fat guy with glasses who was shaking uncontrollably.

There were two rows of bunk beds going down the cell, and the farther down you followed the bunks, the more hardened the faces became. Some inmates wore bright orange uniforms, and someone said that those were the ones that stayed locked up for months or years. There were inmates doing push-ups in the back, others just sat around talking, and some read brightly colored paperbacks.

It was Habib's first time in prison, and he could see just from first impressions that all the information on the inside was hearsay. The guards told the inmates what they wanted to hear, but it wasn't necessarily true. The big question among the newly-arrived was when they would be released. Then some people started talking about having to go in front of a judge before even being considered for release, but no one seemed to know when that would occur either.

A young Hispanic man who sat next to Habib at the picnic table asked him if he was caught drunk driving. Yes, Habib said, I got caught on Eight Street. The man smiled. He said that it seemed like most people here were either caught for drunk driving or having suspended licenses. I went to dinner with my boss, said the man, and I think we drank a little too much wine. What's two bottles between two guys? On my way home I felt fine but I got caught on Sweet Water. The streetlights seemed to be out and before I knew it, red and blue lights were shining behind me. So I pulled over to the side, and brother, the man said, as soon as the cop flashed his light on my face he told me to step out of the car. I knew I was fucked then. My name is Javier, said the man. My name is Habib, he said, shaking his hand.

The rule of the prison phone was that you were only allowed collect calls to landlines and not cell phones. Lucky for Habib, he was one of the last in his group of friends to get a cell phone, so he still remembered most of his friend's home numbers.

He called his other best friend, Snyder Coleman, to see if he could get a hold of Sebastian, who didn't have a house phone. When Snyder accepted the collect call from the operator, Habib told him a shortened version of the story. Snyder Coleman initially felt bad, but he also found it humorous, although he didn't tell Habib that.

Habib asked Snyder to call Sebastian on his cell phone so he could bail him out. Snyder did three-way calling, and the three friends discussed the situation. *You got arrested?* said Sebastian. Can you bail me out? Habib asked, sounding despondent. *Yes, but you won't be getting out until much later. For real,* said Snyder. *That's what happened when I got arrested,* replied Sebastian. *It takes a while from the time you pay the bail to when you get released.* I'll pay you back, Habib said, I'm good for it. Sebastian told him not to worry about it and then said goodbye and hung up.

After the line went silent, Snyder came back on. *What about your father?* Can you call him for me? *No way,* said Snyder Coleman. *It should be you, Habib. He'll be less worried hearing it from you.* You're right, Habib said. Habib then told him that he would call him back later, and they both hung up.

He stared at the phone before dialing his father's number. His chest began to ache because he knew he'd be heartbroken. He quickly dialed the number and his father picked up. Habib told him to accept the call from the operator. *Where are you?* his father said. *It's nine in the morning.* Listen, Habib said, I got arrested. *You what?* I got arrested for drunk driving. *What the hell were you thinking? Who's gonna get you out now, huh? I got no money. You know I have no money! How could you do this to me? You're nothing but trouble!*

Dad, can you take it easy? Sebastian is going to bail me out. *No! No! Fuck Sebastian! You're in prison because of him. No, I'm calling your sister. Your lousy friends can all go to hell. Don't you know I have a weak heart, Habib? Don't you know that?* Please, don't call her. Sebastian is going to pay the bail. Listen to me. *No, Habib, you listen to me. I am calling your sister.* But Sebastian is already on his way to pay the bail. *Fuck Sebastian. He can go to hell with all his money. Your good-for-nothing friends. I blame them, every single one of them. Why don't you listen to me?* But Dad, Habib said in a broken voice. *No. I'm calling your sister right now and she will get you out. Your sister will fix all this.* Then his father said goodbye and hung up the phone.

Habib put his head down against the wall. He stood in that position for a long minute before he felt a presence behind him. It was Javier. Can I ask you a favor? he said. Yes, Habib said. Can you get one of your friends to call my girlfriend on her cell phone? he asked. I have all my numbers on my cell. I got no one else man. Her number is the only one I remember. Habib said don't worry about it, and dialed Snyder Coleman.

Snyder did a three-way call with Javier's girlfriend who only spoke Spanish, and tried his best to translate that her boyfriend was in jail for drunk driving.

After the call was made, and all the important information was given to Javier's girlfriend regarding his whereabouts, both men went back and sat at the out-of-place picnic table by the front of the cell.

Thanks again, man, said Javier. Jail fucking sucks, doesn't it? Yes, it does, Habib said, smiling.

Then all the inmates got up from their bunks and started forming the lunch line. Even if an inmate wasn't hungry, they still had to make a line. Habib and Javier gave their bologna sandwiches with mustard to an inmate that was running a lunch racket in the back corner behind a bunk bed.

Seven hours later all the newly-arrived were taken in front of a judge. They made a single-file line, and each waited their turn patiently. When it was Habib's turn, he stood in shame with legs trembling. He saw his sister through a video monitor, standing in another room answering the judge's terse questioning. Habib did not have to plead innocent or guilty at that time, but instead was quickly processed.

When they got back to the cell, Habib asked Javier about the judge's statement that if the defendant was not a citizen of the United States and was found guilty, he was in danger of being deported. It doesn't mean anything, Javier said, don't worry. But we could get deported, said Habib. Aren't you nervous? All you have to do, Javier said, is hire a good lawyer and that's it, you'll be fine. We're not like these people. We are different, we aren't criminals.

Then at six o'clock the guards started calling the names of the inmates set to be released. Habib and Javier heard their names at 7:30 p.m. As they were led out of the cell in small groups, everyone's spirits suddenly lifted. We are almost there, Javier said.

They were taken down to the first floor of the prison and led into another smaller cell. The cell was dirty and already filled with other inmates. There was graffiti on the walls, and the inmates that were already there seemed angrier than the ones in the previous cell. Most of these inmates were standing. The walls were yellow and the few benches that were in the cell were in an advanced state of decay. To the left of Habib and Javier, there was a very small room with two benches. They saw two older black men sitting on one of the benches in the small room and decided to go sit in that section, which seemed dirtier by comparison to the main part of the cell, but still less crowded.

They sat across from the two Black men and eavesdropped on the conversation. The two men were hunched down, facing each other with their hands in front of them like they were in the middle of a prayer.

He livin' up in Tallahassee now, said the older man. *That's a good thing,* said the younger man, *good for them.* He followed her there all the way from up in Wisconsin after she ran off with his little boy. *I never knew that.* Yes, he told me he was sitting at a bar trying not to give a damn about what she had done. He was celebrating that they were out of his life, he knew he was a no-good father. *Really?* said the younger man, looking disgusted. *He was celebrating? That's some shit.* And he was trying to pick up a woman with his "sad" story, you know, trying to get in her pants crying crocodile tears like they call them. Then he noticed as he's talking to this very fine woman that his crocodile tears were turning into real tears. And then, without saying a word to her, he walked out of that place, leaving that fine woman talking to herself. He got in his El Camino and drove straight down to Tallahassee, only stopping for gas.

During that brief pause in their conversation, an even younger inmate walked in escorted by a guard who told him to sit. The inmate sat next to Habib and Javier. The two Black men looked at him. The young inmate rubbed his eyes and gave a big sigh. *Oh man*, he said, shaking his head.

What's wrong with you? asked the older man that had been telling the story. The young inmate, who looked like a boy, stood up and breathed in and out deeply. *This is it for me*, the boyish inmate said. What you mean? the older man said. *I done been locked up for three years. I never thought I would see this day.* Good Lord, said the older man. *I don't even know what I'm gonna do or how I'm even going to get home. I ain't got no money, I ain't got no phone. I don't even remember my momma's number.* Two years, that's some shit boy, said the other man that had been listening to the story. *I never thought I was gonna last*, said the boyish inmate.

Now you listen, said the older man, you just go and get on that bus, and you tell that driver that you just got released, and you ain't got no money or nothing except the clothes on your back, and to please give you a ride. He should give you a ride. Just what a good Christian should do. *And what if he ain't Christian?* asked the other man. That don't matter, said the older man. How can you not take pity on this young man? It doesn't necessarily take a Christian to have a good heart. Or do it? *Perhaps not*, the other man said.

By this time, despite their age difference, the two Black men had become identical to Habib.

Look here, the older man said, the bus driver will not deny you. You can even ask him to give you his address and promise to pay him back. Blessed are the meek, for they shall inherit the earth. *That's right*, said the other man.

Then the guards began to process the inmates. Everyone was asked to move to the front and middle of the cell. When the metal door opened, all their eyes grew wide as if they had just been allowed entrance through the pearly gates.

Habib's sister Farah was waiting for him outside the prison. Javier's girlfriend was standing next to her. After they made one more line to get their belongings, Habib and Javier exchanged numbers and promised to call each other. They never saw each other again after that.

On the car ride home Habib did not mention the dream about the bombs or his plans to go to Norway. The drive was mostly silent, each trying to avoid the elephant in the room. When they got to his father's apartment in Little Havana, she told him to come over to her house on Sunday. You are selfish, she said. You only care about yourself and going out and getting drunk. When are you going to get serious about your life, Habib? Habib didn't say anything.

He stepped out of the car and his sister drove off leaving him standing in front of the three-story building. When he took his first step towards the building, a boy in a bicycle clipped him, almost knocking him down. Watch where you're going, Habib, the kid yelled. After regaining his footing, he continued to his father's apartment to find him drunk in the kitchen while crying on the phone. Habib's father, Habib bin Hazeem, told the person he was talking to that his son had just arrived and that he would call them back.

That was your aunt, his father said. *She is very disappointed in you. Why do you do these things to me, Habib? You know I have a bad back and can't work. I am an invalid. Do you resent me because of that? Are you ashamed of your father?* Habib put his head down. He couldn't look at his father, so he just stood in the same spot not knowing how to react. *You don't have to answer me, but I want you to think about my questions. Come on, I will get you your dinner. I'm sure you're hungry.* His father served him fried chicken with microwave rice, and sat down to watch him eat. *My own son in prison,* his father said. *I have been crying all day, asking myself, what did I do wrong? Because it's my fault you are the way you are. But I also know that you grew up without a mother. And a boy needs his mother. And I am sorry for that Habib. I apologize to both you and your sister.*

With his plates to the side Habib finally looked at his father and the old man began to glow like the moon does on a clear night. His hair was white and his eyes had bags under them. He had lost his color because he hardly went out anymore. And sometimes, he could barely get out of bed and Habib was no longer sure if it was the alcoholism or the depression. Habib didn't know what to do because he refused to go to a doctor, so they both pretended like things were fine and that this was normal. Habib didn't move out because he knew it would kill him. If his father had no one, especially his children, he would just die. The depression would kill him slowly, but the alcoholism could get to him first. Or was that all a fantasy that he was spinning to himself? Habib wondered.

What if we just leave, Habib said. Can't we just go somewhere else? *What do you mean leave?* his father asked. *Where do you want to go?* I have a friend that lives in Oslo, Norway. He can help me find a job and a place to live. *You want to go to Norway?* Habib bin Hazeem asked. *Why do you want to go to Norway? Why in the world would you want to go there? You spend one night in jail and you're already getting crazy ideas.* A change of your surroundings. Don't you think we could start over somewhere else? *No, you need to get some rest. You've had a long night, Habib. You are talking nonsense.*

That night Habib bin Habib dreamt again about the bombs falling over Miami. The image was clearer. In this dream he could focus on each bomb individually. And it was this way he recognized that out of the dozens of bombs falling, each was slightly different from the rest.

Some were shaped differently and others were darker than the ones before them. And there were some that seemed damaged or bent. But they all still fell in the same way over houses, cars, banks, skyscrapers, schools, the Miami river, Miami Beach, downtown, and little Havana. In the dream, Miami was covered by a blanket of falling bombs. Habib never saw the aftermath but just the continuous bombing and a sense of dread from the anticipation of what was to come, but by then he would wake up.

That Saturday Habib went to a picnic with his Vietnamese friend Tinh. Habib first met Tinh while playing football in high school. Their friendship was mostly based on sports and fishing. He had been invited the week before and he decided at the last minute to go. Tinh said he would pick him up. The picnic was at the beach in Key Biscayne. Tinh's family was all there. They had barbeque pork, and everyone ate and talked.

An hour later, all the adults and kids decided to go in the water. Habib told Tinh that he didn't really feel like going in. In reality, he didn't want to go in because of his body; he was self conscious about his skinny body and tattoos. Despite this, Tinh made him take off his T-shirt and go in the water with the rest of the family. They had to walk far out just to get to the sandbar.

They all lay back in the warm water. The kids splashed around and played. Habib laid his head back, feeling the warm water on the back of his neck. He closed his eyes and listened to the waves crashing, the children laughing, and the grownups swimming.

Habib raised his head from the water and asked Tinh, who was floating next to him, if he had ever thought about living in another country. *What you mean?* Tinh asked. *My family's here. Why would I wanna live anywhere else?* What about Vietnam? Haven't you ever wanted to go see what it's like over there now? Tinh moved his arms side to side over the water. *Vietnam, I don't want to go back there. There's nothing there. Maybe to visit and get me a wife, but that's it.* But what if something happened here, and you and your family had to go somewhere else. *I don't know. Why you always gotta ask stupid questions, Habib?*

Then Tinh seemed to be thinking about his answer carefully. *I guess I'd go to Hawaii. I hear they got good fishing there. And I always wanted to go there.* What about a country like Norway? *Norway?* asked Tinh. *I don't know about Norway. What's in Norway? Ain't it cold in Norway?* I like the cold, said Habib. It's nice there, 'specially the capital, Oslo. *Oslo? Norway? Cuz, what you talking about? Aren't there Vikings and shit? You gonna freeze in Norway, Habib. Not me, I like the tropics. I hate the cold. Cuz, you crazy.*

The women are beautiful in Norway, Habib said. *We getting ready to get out of the water,* said Tinh. *Let's go! You hungry?* I'm still full. *What you talking about full? We got more watermelon! And we still got chicken and ribs!*

By the time the sun was on its way down, and everyone had eaten almost everything, Tinh's clan started packing up for the ride back. Habib never mentioned the arrest for drunk driving. He wasn't sure if it was because he was ashamed or because he just didn't feel like going over the whole incident again. In the end, on the ride home, Habib gave up in convincing Tinh about moving to Norway. That night, as he lay in bed, listening to his father snore in the next room, he thought he was losing the ambition to move his entire world into another country. He felt like he was running out of time.

The next day Habib went to his sister's house in North Miami. In the beginning, they talked about a lot of things, and like most days, they only skimmed the surface of the real issue. When it was dinner time, Habib sat at the table with his two little nephews and brother-in-law, Juan. Eventually, after everyone was finished with their dinner, everything was unloaded.

He's an alcoholic, Farah said. *We have that in our genes, Habib. It's like a dormant monster inside us, and you're heading down the same path. Our father is lost. He needs to get help. I have a family to worry about, Habib. I don't have time to go partying like you. I have responsibilities*, she said while feeding the youngest. *Why do you think I won't let him stay here when he's on one of his benders?* But he's your dad too. *I know, but he's a drunk.* He's a sloppy drunk, Habib said. He's harmless. He gets drunk because you ignore him. Because you're ashamed of him. *Why are you giving him excuses?* Farah asked.

Farah's husband Juan usually stayed quiet during these family discussions. Habib got along with him, but he didn't have a backbone and never stood up to Farah.

Do you realize, Habib, that he is a child? Farah asked pointedly. *We have to take charge of him because he is a mess and can't take care of himself. We are his parents now and that's not right.*

Do you see how things have turned completely upside down? We don't deserve this, Habib. And guess what will happen when he dies? Guess. I don't know, Habib said. *We will inherit his $80,000 debt. That's what's going to happen. Imagine that. Can you afford to have that much debt, Habib? Because I know I can't. I have two kids to raise. When that man dies, that will be his legacy to us. And all because of a woman that he refuses to forget about.* Habib couldn't recognize his own sister. So you want to ignore him? Habib asked.

She saw herself in Habib's weary eyes, and then she snapped out of it. *I'm sorry that you have to be the one stuck with him, but he has to be taught a lesson. He needs to do something for himself. We can't take care of him forever. Do you really think that I want my kids to have a relationship with an alcoholic? You are on your way there too, Habib. So please stop for one second and think about your future. You're a dropout for god's sake. And please, I really don't want to hear any more of this nonsense about Norway. You need to wake up and open your eyes to reality. You need to go back to school.*

Many years later, Habib bin Habib al Fulan will brave the cold and snow of December in Oslo to meet a friend in Frogner Park.

He will wait for him in the center of the park, right by the fountain. As he waits, while sitting on a park bench, he will watch people go about their lives. He will see lovely couples, tired office workers, pretty blond women smiling amidst the cold, seeing their own breath rise.

He will see a young Asian man fighting the freezing wind. The young man will give it a valiant effort while covered up in many layers of clothing. It will remind Habib of his own brave effort against the insipid, endearing climate when he first stepped off the plane. And Habib will think how curious it was that he caught a cold during his first week in Oslo. The cold wouldn't go away, and before he knew it, he had a high fever. His roommate, John Voorten, had to drag him to a clinic against his will. At the clinic, a doctor by the name of Hamsun told him he had pneumonia and prescribed him antibiotics, advising him to drink lots of liquids and get plenty of rest. The doctor told Habib that these trans-Atlantic flights are like germ incubators, adding that they zap all the energy out of a healthy person, leaving them vulnerable with their defenses down.

That night, with John Voorten keeping a close watch over him, Habib had a dream. At exactly five minutes past midnight, when his fever was at its highest point, the dream began with an image of bombs falling over a distant Miami. As the dream continued, he realized that he was no longer scared watching the bombs drop, but paying close atten-tion, he saw the bombs uncurl and turn into people. These people came down landing on their feet like cats, absorbing the impact in their knees and then standing upright. In this dream, Habib noticed that the people were of all shapes and sizes, and he recognized some of them. He saw his father uncurling from the shape of an H-bomb and land with a thud. He saw his sister Farah and her husband too. And not far behind them, he saw his two little nephews land with big smiles on their faces. Then Habib saw one bomb transform into Sebastian Montes right before reaching the ground. His old friend landed on his feet, kneeling, then he turned upright and walked away. After that he saw Tinh and his family falling. There were many of them, and they all fell in good humor, laughing and united. Habib even saw Javier and his girlfriend uncurl into themselves from two portly gray bombs. At this point in the dream, he recognized almost all of the people. They were all there—his family, friends, and acquaintances—even people he had seen in the streets and in bars. But despite who they were, they all fell as bombs, then after landing on their feet, walked away like clay figures brought to life.

La Femme

She was smiling when she told him, but the words had a numbing effect by the time they reached his ears. They were sitting on a white leather sofa in their living room, and she was wearing a yellow dress with thin straps that illuminated her smooth, brown shoulders. Her dark hair, like a wild horse's mane, went *way* down her back and he remembered thinking that she had the prettiest hair of any girl that he had ever loved.

"Are you listening to me?"

"No."

"It's not that I stopped loving you," she said.

"But you just said that you don't love me. Why did you stop?"

She looked at his face and the answer was in her eyes. Then he felt a knot in his chest.

"I was never *in* love with you, Habib," she said. He didn't say anything, and she continued.

"I think I was in love with the idea of a new life with you, or the life you could give me."

"What about the kid?"

"You will always be the father of the kid."

"I don't understand," he said. "Are you having an affair?"

"There is someone, but it doesn't matter. He has nothing to do with this. I tried to pretend to love you, but it was unhealthy for me and you and for the kid."

"Tessa is staying with me."

"Can we please be civil?"

"Who built your family's house in *Cotui*? It was me and my money. Your family has the biggest house in the ghetto because of me."

She didn't say anything.

"I love you Oona. Think about what you're doing."

"No, I've already decided. There's nothing to think about."

He got down on his knees and begged her. When the tears started coming out of his eyes, she stood up and with the skirt of the yellow dress waving like a cape behind her, she marched to the front door. He followed her and watched her get into a black Mercedes Benz being driven by a small man with a shaved head, a Charlie Chaplin mustache, and aviator sunglasses.

After she was gone, he went to the bathroom and washed his face. He looked at himself in the mirror; his eyes were red and his nose was stuffy. At one o'clock, he got in his car and went to pick up his daughter from school. It was the start of the holiday weekend, and they drove from school straight to McDonald's like he had promised her in the morning. He got her a Happy Meal and ordered a cheeseburger with fries for himself. They sat on a table right next to the indoor playground. Tessa ate her nuggets slowly while playing with the toys that came with the meal. He gazed at his daughter who was lovely and angelic in the fishtail braids her mother had sent her off to school in. He wasn't totally alone, at least he still had the kid, he thought.

"Is Mom gonna meet us?" his daughter said.

"Not right now, sweetie, but maybe later."

As soon as he said that, he imagined her mother getting stabbed repeatedly by a tall figure in a green ski mask. Let's not get angry, he thought, for the sake of the kid. And besides, he remembered reading somewhere child psychologists saying kids can sense every—sense e-v-e-r-y-t-h-i-n-g.

The next day, a Saturday, they went to the grocery store. The store was empty except for a dark-haired woman with a little boy. His daughter sat in the shopping cart, and as he got closer to the produce section, he noticed a body hanging from the ceiling. He wasn't sure if he was seeing things or if it was an actual body. The closer he pushed the cart, the more scared he felt, for the body hanging by the neck was of his wife. Then he asked himself honestly if he was seeing things or if this was wish fulfillment fantasies? He was way too resentful. First murder and now suicide. The body hung limp, almost stiff, and she wore the same yellow dress that now resembled a tattered flag. He wanted to get on a step ladder and bring it down, but instead he just pushed the cart towards the grapes.

"I want the purple grapes, Daddy," his daughter said.

"But Daddy likes the green ones."

"No, purple."

When they went for the bananas, that's when they were directly below the body of his wife. He noticed no blood. He looked at her Jimmy Choo shoes, and he was positive that he was seeing things nobody else could see. Was it the future? Was it a ghost?

"What are you looking at, Daddy?"

"Nothing, let's just grab these bananas. Do you also want tangerines, honey?"

"Let's get some chocolate ice cream."

"Okay, let's get some ice cream."

He pushed the shopping cart away from the produce section almost in slow motion. When he turned into the freezer aisle, he could still feel his wife's body hanging from the ceiling. The dark-haired woman passed him going the opposite way, giving him a penetrating stare like if she had just seen OJ Simpson shopping at Kmart.

After getting home, putting everything away, watching a Disney movie with his kid and finally taking her to bed, Habib stepped outside to his driveway to smoke a cigarette.

Across the street, his neighbor Miguel Santiago was staring at the moon hiding behind the clouds.

"Hello Habib, how's it going?"

"I'm doing okay, sneaking a cigarette, how about you?"

"Molly left."

"Again?"

"Yeah, she said it's for good this time. I know she's at his house, but you know what? I don't care anymore," he said and walked over to Habib.

He was half Jamaican and Puerto Rican, and his face had the broken lines of a much older man. His smile kept breaking, but he kept trying to maintain his pleasant demeanor.

"The way I see it," he said, putting his right hand on his chest, "I will let go. She doesn't belong to me anymore. Life is too short. If my love is not enough for her, then it's okay, I can live with that. But I sure hope the kids stay with me. I need the kids, you know?"

Habib threw the unfinished cigarette on the floor, stepped on it, and crossed his arms.

"I saw Oona leave yesterday," Miguel said.

"It's what she wants. I thought about going after her, but what's the point?"

"Can you believe these women? And we are fools for loving them. We continue to love them despite their faults. But that's love. I love my wife so much. And I'm sure you love your wife too."

"I think I do. I'm not even sure anymore."

Miguel looked at Habib with the hollow eyes of a man who'd survived a trek through the desert. "You have just spoken the unspoken truth," he said and turned around to go back to his house.

That night Habib could still smell his wife's scent in their king-sized bed. He turned towards her side of the bed and pictured her there; he felt like he had a missing limb. Why is she always wearing that yellow dress? he whispered to himself in the darkness. He closed his eyes and tried to stop thinking about violent things happening to her in the yellow dress.

On Sunday morning they went to a park next to a canal that leads to the sea. He saw his wife's body floating face down. They were having a picnic and he had to stand up to get a good view; it was definitely her and she was wearing the same dress, but her hair was coming off in tufts.

"What's wrong, Daddy?"

"Nothing, baby, I was just looking to see if there was any fish in the canal."

"Are we gonna try to catch a catfish?"

"Yes, of course," he said grabbing their fishing pole.

They walked over to the canal, and he flung the rod trying to fish his wife out, but he couldn't get the hook on her.

"I wanna try, Daddy."

"Hold on, honey, Daddy needs to try to bring this in."

"There's some fishy right there. What are you doing?"

He tried once more to hook the body, but it was useless, and it continued to drift and then it sank until he couldn't see it anymore. He gave up and handed the rod to his daughter. As soon as she cast the rod, she had a bite, and he helped her pull in a very curious looking green fish with black vertical stripes. It was too small though, so they had to throw it back.

When they arrived home, the neighborhood was full of police cruisers and an ambulance. Habib drove slowly and followed a police officer's instructions to stop.

"Excuse me, sir," the police officer began. "You're going to have to turn around if you're not a resident."

"I *am* a resident. I live in that house right there. What's going on?"

"There was a murder-suicide at the house across the street. Did you know your neighbor, sir?"

"Yes, that's Miguel's house. What happened?"

"Your neighbor just gunned down his entire family. We're going to have to ask you some questions before we can let you through. Can you pull over?"

"Please keep it down. My daughter is in the back."

"What's happening?"

"Everything is fine, honey. There was an accident. That's all, but everything is going to be okay. Daddy just has to pull over and talk to the officer for a minute."

"Just pull over here," the police officer said, pointing to the side of the street.

Habib pulled over and talked to the officer, telling him everything he knew about Miguel Santiago. He told him they were friendly, but not exactly friends, and that their kids sometimes played together. And yes, he was aware of their marital discord. The last time he spoke to Miguel was yesterday, and they talked about his wife. Or at least Miguel talked about his wife and Habib just listened. And no, he did not seem angry, he seemed relieved. No, he didn't know of Miguel owning any guns. Yes, Habib said, he will contact the detective if he can think of anything else that might assist in their investigation.

He put his daughter to bed in the early evening without explaining to her the incident. He didn't go in front of his house because the cops were still there, but instead went to his backyard to smoke a cigarette. Despite standing under the shadow of his mango tree, chain smoking for a long while, he didn't see his wife anywhere and couldn't even clearly see her in his mind's eye. There was one moment where he thought he saw someone walking away, but he didn't bother to investigate it. She wasn't there anymore. She wasn't dead. She wasn't alive. She was just gone. Miguel stole his anger and apparently used it on his own wife and kids. Habib was beat now; he almost had no purpose without the anger.

In the morning, he awoke from a dream that he couldn't remember to discover his daughter's flat hand resting on his forehead. She was sitting cross-legged on the bed right next to him in her Sponge Bob pajamas, watching him.

"Daddy, you were talking in your sleep."

"I was," he said raising himself to sit up. He put his hand on hers. "Are you hungry?"

"Yes, I want pancakes."

"Let's go make some pancakes then."

They both got off the bed and went to the kitchen to start breakfast. He grabbed two bowls from the cupboard. She sat on a stool next to the counter and watched him get the flour, milk, and eggs ready. He sifted together the baking powder, the flour, and salt. He then grabbed the second bowl and mixed the eggs and milk together, finally adding in the flour mix, and stirred it. Once it was smooth enough, he stirred in the butter.

"How about blueberries?"

"Yes, please," she said, while resting her small chin on the knuckles of her hands leaning in close to his face.

After getting the blueberries from the fridge and washing them in the sink, he mixed them in and continued stirring the batter. He poured a little vegetable oil into a pan, and let it heat up for about ten minutes before pouring the batter in to form a large pancake.

"Can we go to the zoo today?"

"Sure, we can go to the zoo."

"Is that where they have the manatees?"

"No, honey, the manatees are at the Seaquarium."

"Then let's go to there. I want to see the manatees."

Habib flipped the large, golden pancake which kind of reminded him of a giant yellow sun expanding, ready to engulf a planet. So this is how worlds perish, he said, mostly whispering to himself.

"Daddy, are you listening to me?"

"Yes."

Leaving for Paris

In the fall of 2009, Doofy went out on two very different dates. The first date wasn't really a date. The girl was a prostitute, but he got more than his money's worth and ended up spending time with a really nice person.

The date took place at a hotel in Fort Lauderdale that was located some thirty miles from where he lived with his mother in Miami. He first saw the ad on Craigslist, and despite his infatuation with the Black girl in the ad (he couldn't believe that she was really a prostitute because she was just too beautiful), he did not try to contact her. Since he was going through a drought, was still single at thirty-two, and had no real prospects, he continued to frequent the website by telling himself that he was doing it just to look at the photos. But he was lying to himself, because he knew deep down that if he encountered the right girl, with the right price, and the right photograph, he would take a chance.

He ran into the same girl's ad on two more occasions while searching for other escorts. It almost seemed like she was calling out to him. In the ad, there were three different photos of her. In the first photo she was sitting on a big, overwhelming wicker chair, wearing a short purple dress that showed off her long legs. In the second photo, she was standing in the doorway of a hotel bathroom, wearing a white nightgown with a generous view of her cleavage. And in the third photo, she was sitting on a hotel bed with a soft, beaming smile, in a tight "I'm in Miami Bitch" T-shirt and wearing blue jeans that fit her like a glove. That third photo was Doofy's favorite. He liked it because it made her look like the typical girl next door. He ended up saving all three photos to his hard drive and saved her number to his cell phone. The price was right but he still had to convince himself.

He made up his mind one night while drinking three pitchers of beer and four shots of tequila with a fellow bag boy at a local bar near his mother's apartment in South Miami. He didn't tell his co-worker what he was going to do, but there came a point after the third or fourth shot of tequila when a light bulb lit up above his head. From then on, he was on a mission like a drug addict looking for a fix.

On the short walk home, he called her. Her name was Virginia, and the phone rang three times before a smooth, sexy voice answered.

"Hello?"

"Hi."

"Can I help you?"

"Um, yes, um, I was calling about your ad."

"Are you looking for a date?"

Doofy sighed heavily as he walked the three blocks to his mother's apartment. Fear and sex amalgamated in his mind.

"Hello? Are you there?"

"Yes, I'm sorry. Yes, I would like to see you."

"Are you drunk?"

"I'm a little tipsy, but I have to tell you I think you're the most beautiful girl I have ever seen."

"Thank you so much. I'm so flattered. What's your name?"

"My name is Yuniesky. Yuniesky Zabala."

"What?"

"Yuniesky Zabala."

"What kind of name is that?"

"I'm Cuban but my grandparents on my father's side are Russian. I was named after my grandfather."

"Wow, that's very interesting."

"Yes, I know. I'm a mutt. Have you ever been with a mutt?"

"Yes, Yuniesky, I've been with lots of Mutts, you won't be my first."

There was a pause, and then he heard her breathing and he pictured her at home in bed. "It's kind of late tonight, Yuniesky. Would you like to meet tomorrow?"

"Sure. Yes, of course. Definitely."

"How about in the early evening, say around six or seven?"

"That's perfect. Where do you stay at?"

"I have a place in Fort Lauderdale where I like to meet clients, it's right on Commercial Blvd. Call me tomorrow around four to confirm, and I'll give you the details, sweetie."

"Okay, I will."

"You have a good night now, Yuniesky Zabala, and be safe please."

"I will. Thank you. It was a pleasure meeting you."

"It was a pleasure meeting *you*."

"The pleasure is all mine."

She giggled like a schoolgirl. "Sweet dreams, honey." They both hung up at the same time.

Early the next evening Doofy drove to the hotel where the

date was to take place. Just parking his car made him nervous. He imagined that she was an undercover police officer and that this was a sting. He stayed in the car fixing his hair, clearing it away from his face; it was dirty blond, long in the front and short at the back. Some people said he looked like Kurt Cobain's long lost retarded brother. He then smelled himself and sprayed more cologne. He inspected his shirt closely.

After ten minutes and despite his paranoia, Doofy finally got out of his car and walked into the hotel lobby. She was in room 403. When he caught the elevator, a short man in a white suit with a shaved head, thin mustache, and aviator sunglasses was already there. The man asked him what floor:

"What floor, papa?"

Doofy said four please.

"There are only three floors, papa."

Doofy looked at the buttons on the elevator. He panicked. "The third floor then," he said, looking bewildered.

He got off on the third floor and walked down the hall. He stopped in front of room 303 and called Virginia with his cell phone.

"Hello, Virginia," he said, as a long lock of his hair fell over his face. "Hey sweetie, where you at?"

"I'm at the hotel, but there's no fourth floor. Are you sure you didn't mean room 303?" Virginia started laughing hysterically.

"Oh my God," she said, trying to get a word in between laughs, "you're at the wrong hotel."

"You said the Lindon. I'm at the Lindon."

"No, there are two Lindons, honey. That's the regular Lindon. I told you the Lindon Suites. Baby, that's why I told you to make a left on Commercial."

"I just heard Lindon and I saw it on the right."

"Oh my God! This is so funny! You are so cute!"

"But why are there two Lindons so close to each other? That doesn't make sense."

"One is the suites and the one where you're at is just a regular hotel."

Doofy laughed while his face turned red like an apple, but he was relieved because he felt that no cop would laugh at him like she did. Or maybe they still would but might feel pity for him and let him go. He went back to his car and drove to the correct Lindon hotel. When he finally made it to the fourth floor, he stood in front of the door, breathing deeply.

He knocked on the door and when it opened, a beautiful Black girl with hazel eyes and a curvaceous figure was standing before him. She looked exactly like the photos from Craigslist but better. Doofy was a little bit at ease now, but her beauty overtook him. She was wearing a purple nightgown.

"Hello," she said, smiling and letting him in.

"Finally made it. I got freaked out back there for a little bit. No fourth floor. It was like *The Twilight Zone*."

Virginia started laughing again. She had a good, hearty laugh that was still girlish with all the right pauses.

"You are so sexy," Doofy said.

"Thank you," she said, grabbing his hand and closing the door. They went and sat on the bed.

"I'm just bad with directions, and I made sure to leave early. But when you told me the hotel name, I ignored every other piece of information you gave me because I knew where it was. But I didn't know that there were two of them so close to each other."

"Yes, there are," she said, looking into his eyes. "Why don't you get comfortable?"

"Okay," Doofy said, unbuttoning his shirt.

He then stood up and took off his shoes and pants. He stood in front of her in blue boxer briefs and black socks looking as pale as the moon.

"Come here you silly boy," she said, grabbing his arm and pulling him toward her on the bed.

Virginia kissed him. He lay in the bed with her. She still had her night gown on, and they continued kissing. They stopped for a moment and looked at each other. He smiled and she laughed.

"You are so beautiful," he said, studying her face.

"Thank you." He caressed her left cheek. "You're so funny," she said.

"I try," he said. "I actually went into the wrong hotel because I knew it would be funny."

"You wanted to break the ice."

"Yes, that was the plan."

He kissed her again deeply and with hunger, and then they both fell into the perennial act of making love. Much later, after they were done and just lying naked and in each other's arms, they smoked a joint that she found at the bottom of her purse. It was at that point they began to talk about their dreams and their families.

Doofy wanted to move to Paris like the writer Henry Miller. He was thinking of taking French classes at FIU in order to motivate himself toward his goal. He didn't tell Virginia this, but he believed that he would find the love of his life once he got there. Virginia wanted to save enough money to open a salon in a high traffic area in Midtown

Miami. Her friends were already paying her to do their hair, so why not open up her own business and finally grow up.

That's all she wanted to do, was to be herself and have her own money without answering to anyone.

When they spoke about family, she told Doofy about her estranged father and how he showed up, on odd-numbered years, asking for money. He was a man that she really wanted to hate but couldn't. And Doofy in turn told her about how he took care of his mother who suffered from a deep depression. He knew that it stemmed from a broken heart, but he had no idea how to help her mend it.

They changed the subject when the mood turned sad and instead talked about the funny people they knew and funny situations they had been in. After Doofy finished telling her about doing mushrooms in Miami Beach with his friends Sebastian and Lee, Virginia perked up, naked and beautiful, and recounted a story about a house party she had attended once where some guy grabbed his girlfriend, who was a tiny girl, and threw her in the trunk of his car because she was nagging him too much. The guy returned to the party where he did a lot of drugs for the rest of the night. When he finally left, he drove away drunk and high with his girlfriend still in the trunk. On the drive home, he crashed violently into a canal off Krome Avenue, where he drowned while his girlfriend survived after being ejected from the trunk of the vehicle. Doofy listened carefully to every word, and when she was done, asked her if he could use it for a future story he wanted to write, and she said yeah, of course you can.

"Are you a writer?"

"Yes," he said.

Then they took a shower together and made love for a second time. After that, he got dressed, paid her, and left.

* * *

The second date that Doofy went on was two weeks later, and it was a real date, meaning that he didn't have to pay the girl to spend time with him. The girl's name was Klarissa and she worked as a dental hygienist at a clinic in Homestead. She was short, delicate, and pretty and the sound of her voice made Doofy swoon. And even though she claimed to be Filipino, she was really American. He met her through a friend and his wife, who were visiting from Seattle. They were at a club celebrating his friend's wife's birthday and Doofy danced with Klarissa the entire night. He kissed her softly, and even though it wasn't a French kiss, it felt magical nevertheless. He got her number and promised to call.

Doofy called her the next day and they made a date for Sunday. When Sunday came, he got lost on the way to her house because he had written the address wrong. As a result, he arrived late and they were supposed to see a movie, but they figured they could catch the next show.

"I'm bad with directions," Doofy said.

"And I thought I was bad," Klarissa said.

They sat on her couch. Klarissa was watching the movie *Hitch* starring Will Smith. "Have you seen *Hitch*?"

"I've seen like half of it. I'm always catching part of it on cable."

Doofy didn't really like Hitch; he thought it was stupid. He felt strange watching it. He put his arm behind Klarissa on the couch. She grabbed her laptop computer that was on a coffee table and went to the Overstock website.

"I want to show you the painting I'm getting for the living room," she said.

Doofy's arm didn't feel right the way he had it placed; he was uncomfortable and he kept fidgeting.

"You see this painting, it has three canvases. I like the dark colors; it's very chaotic. The middle canvas is the darkest. I think it would go good with the green of this wall. What do you think?"

Doofy looked at the painting. He was indifferent to it. "It's cool," he said.

What else was he gonna say?

"What do you think of this one? It's also made up of three separate canvases. It's a rose. I think it's okay. But I want something dark. Something that balances out the room."

Doofy focused hard on the painting. It was a giant red rose with a white background, and he liked it. He liked that it was simple.

He didn't know what to say, so he just kept staring at it. "I don't like it either," she said.

Klarissa put down the laptop computer and they watched the end of the movie. Doofy didn't say much. He was going through one of his quiet moods, and besides, he just wanted to relax and let things take their natural course. But the truth was that he wasn't sure about his intentions anymore. He couldn't put his finger on it, but he also knew that he hadn't been sure about a lot of things in those days. Doofy was turning thirty-three in December, and he was feeling like his life up to that Sunday, on that couch, next to that girl, was a giant question mark. It was a scary feeling to have while sitting next to a pretty girl.

"I guess we should go now," she said, standing up. "Yes, let's go."

Doofy drove to the movie theater that was in a mall not far from Klarissa's apartment.

She wanted to watch a romantic comedy starring an ensemble cast of Hollywood celebrities. Doofy thought she was joking with him.

"What's wrong?"

"Nothing. Let's see it."

They sat and watched the movie and ate popcorn. He laughed at the wrong moments in the film because he didn't really know how to react to a film that was so obviously bad. There were a couple of parts where Doofy's laugh stood out above the rest of the audience and hovered there, like a strange, ironic bat. He laughed during the sad moments in the film for no other reason than that he actually found them funny. And in one part, when a main character runs through security at an airport to catch the love of his life before she gets on the plane, Doofy whispered to Klarissa, if that had been for real, they would have shut down the airport, pummeled Ashton Kutcher down, and sent him to Guantanamo. Klarissa didn't say anything.

After the movie, they went to a pizza restaurant, where Doofy met her roommate who happened to work there as a waitress. The restaurant was getting ready to close, and they waited for her roommate to be let out. While they waited, Klarissa told Doofy about the delicious wings they serve at her favorite bar. Doofy smiled but he was really feeling shitty about spending money on such an awful film. It was against his morals.

When her roommate got off, Doofy drove them to the bar. The bar was a little hole in the wall located in a shopping center not too far from the restaurant. It was dead inside but it felt homely. When they sat at the bar, Klarissa's roommate sat in between Doofy and Klarissa. They ordered drinks and thirty chicken wings. The girls talked about the movie while he listened.

"You said we were going to see that movie together," said Klarissa's roommate. "I can't believe you sold me out."

"I forgot," Klarissa said.

"That's so wrong. Isn't it wrong, Yuniesky?"

"Yes," Doofy said, "that is selling out."

"You see," she said.

"Well I wouldn't mind seeing it again. I'll go with you."

"No, you saw it already. I'll go with Lisa. You already sold me out." The bartender brought the drinks and the wings. Everyone ate and drank.

"So what do you think of the wings," Klarissa said, looking at Doofy from behind her roommate.

"They're very good. I've never had wings with garlic."

"Yeah," said the roommate, "but what makes them really good is the way they marinade them overnight before they grill them."

"Oh, okay," said Doofy, savoring the garlic.

After they ate and their plates were to the side, Klarissa saw a guy that she knew and called him over. Her friend looked like Long Duk Dong from the movie *Sixteen Candles* but with a goatee. Everyone talked and drank some more. Then they followed Long to play darts. It became Doofy and Klarissa's roommate against Klarissa and Long Duk, or Hispanics against Asians. Long Duk had his own darts and Doofy's team lost four games in a row. They then played pool and Doofy and the roommate lost again. Doofy wasn't very good at bar games.

After that, Doofy just sat around by the bar watching Klarissa and Long Duk talk and talk and talk. Then everyone ordered Jagger Bombs. Doofy tried to ignore them by watching a strong man competition on the television.

"Is everything okay," said Klarissa.

"Yes," said Doofy.

"If you're ready to leave, let's leave."

"No, I'm good."

An hour later she came back to Doofy.

"What's up Yuniesky? Are you sure you don't want to go? We can get a ride."

"No, I'm having fun."

"Are you sure?"

"Am I sure of what?"

"Don't you have a long drive?"

"No, I'm fine."

They left two hours later. But right before leaving, Klarissa gave Long Duk Dong, or the man that resembled the character from that classic film, her number. Then Doofy dropped them off, and Klarissa asked him to please text her when he got home.

"Okay," Doofy said, and drove off.

When Doofy got home, he sent her a text message but she never replied.

* * *

The following week Doofy was driving around with his best friend Gabriel trying to best explain the date with Klarissa. They had just eaten at their favorite Middle-Eastern restaurant.

Gabriel was behind the wheel of his brand-new black Mercedes Benz. He had a toothpick hanging from his mouth, and he drove with one hand behind the wheel while simultaneously fixing his hair with the other.

"Rides nice, don't it," he said. "And smell that new car smell."

"It's a good smell," Doofy said.

"But yeah, like I was saying, that's just a damn shame," Gabriel said, while steering on to US 1.

"I really don't care anymore. I wasn't into her anyway."

"What did I tell you about these girls? You gotta man up and represent. You can't be letting them take over the date. You take her where you want to take her. To the restaurant you want. To the nighttime activity you choose. Not the other way around. You gotta lead because that's what a woman wants. A woman wants a man to take control no matter what. You frustrate me, brotha!"

"How do you think I feel?"

"I can't imagine how you feel. You're like the freaking Pope. I don't even remember the last time you were going steady with a chick. How do you do it, brotha?"

"I wake up, I read, I write, I buy a lot of porn. I go to work, I come home, and go to sleep." "Then you must really like *Manolita*. Cause if you're happy with *Manolita*, well fuck it!"

They both started laughing while the pink lit streets of South Miami scrolled past them like a film reel.

"No, I want to break it off with *Manolita*."

Gabriel spread his right hand wide and put it against Doofy's face.

"This is what you love, brotha."

"No," Doofy said. "I want real love."

"See, that's your problem. You can't be talking like that. You can't be thinking all this lovey-dovey shit with these girls. You gotta be real, but for the moment. And in the first moment, it's all S-E-X. Love comes after. Listen to me. Have I ever led you astray with my advice? And not for nothing, I grew up with three sisters, I know females and let me tell you, they're just like us."

"Well how do you want me to be?"

"I'll tell you what you shouldn't be. Don't be doofy."

"What the fuck is doofy?"

"You have a doofy style. Now don't take this the wrong way, but my wife says that sometimes, you come off a little doofy. You need to let your goatee grow out, and get a decent haircut. You gotta be willing to change if you want a chance with these girls, B."

"Your wife said I'm doofy?"

"Yeah, she said you're doofy, and Sebastian dresses gay. That's why the both of you are always having these chick problems. I mean, you don't have to pay it no mind. It don't mean nothing. Then again, that's a woman giving her honest opinion, and maybe you should think about it. You need to change a little B."

"I'm still trying to figure out what doofy means," said Doofy.

"Doofy is a combination of Goofy and Duffus. Goofy and Duffus equal Doofy."

"That's kind of messed up. I'm not even good enough to be just Goofy? I gotta be Doofy? I gotta be a combination?"

"Women know what they're talking about. There's nothing wrong with changing your style a little bit, to a little less Doofy."

So Doofy sat there deflated, contemplating the word Doofy.

* * *

When he went to sleep that night, he had a dream in which the earth shone yellow like the autumn leaves in Central Park. The dream continued in the same manner with the yellow earth spinning for some time, until the vibrant yellows peeled off like the skin of a grapefruit unveiling a vibrant scene set at the Champ de Mars with the Eiffel Tower soaring tall, stabbing the sky like it was an alien rocket that just landed. He was there, sitting on a park bench, wearing a luxurious blue, two-piece suit, and to his genuine surprise, he looked happy. To his right there was a sea of green grass shining like Irish hills; to his left guitarists with black berets performed acoustic versions of French pop songs for lovers. He watched those same lovers stroll past him, holding hands and kissing. He saw himself enjoy the cool, endearing wind as it caressed his face. In the distance, there was a young woman in a pink blouse, denim jacket, and a short skirt heading towards him with loud determination. She was so beautiful that she seemed to be gliding. Then he saw himself stand up to take a deep breath from the wistful European air. The girl heading towards him had long black hair like a gipsy, and her eyes sparkled like two blue stars exhausting themselves in outer space.

The closer she got, the faster she walked, until she jumped on him, hugging him tight, while kissing him on the mouth passionately. With her long, white, delicate arms around him, he began to feel his whole spirit revive.

"I am Morgane," she said softly, by his ear.

We finally meet," he said.

"Yes," she said, smiling and looking at his face.

"I'm Doofy. It's nice to meet you."

"*Excusez-moi?*"

"I mean, I'm Yuniesky."

"I'm sorry, I must go, I have made a mistake."

"No, wait," he said, while trying to hold on to her arm, but she got away.

The girl ran fast, and he was left alone except for a guitarist gravitating towards him, almost creeping, and finally standing next to him. The street performer was playing a giant, red acoustic guitar, and even though he strummed an upbeat tune, there was no smile on his face.

Yuniesky wanted to dunk his head in the sound hole of the guitar. And as he saw himself make a move towards the guitarist, at the very moment he was stooping his head to put it in the sound hole, he awoke on his bed, at his mother's apartment where the morning was gray and there was a strange noise coming from the other side of his bedroom door. Yuniesky sat up listening, trying to discern the sound. It sounded like someone wheezing. He got up from the bed slowly, opened the door, and saw his mother in her pajamas sitting down hunched at the kitchen table trying to breathe. She was huffing and puffing in short breaths.

Yuniesky rubbed his eyes and asked her what was wrong.

"I can't breathe," she said.

"What do you mean, you can't breathe?"

"I was up all night. I just couldn't breathe."

"Get dressed, I'm taking you to the hospital," Yuniesky said, and grabbed a T-shirt that was strewn on a chair in his bedroom and went looking for pants.

When they were both ready, they got in his car and headed in the general direction of the nearest hospital. Yuniesky was aware that it wasn't the best hospital, but it was the closest one. When he got to a red light, he grabbed his cell phone and called his job and told them that he wasn't feeling very well and wasn't coming in.

As he ended the call, his mother sat in the passenger seat looking as pale as a tiny ghost.

Her hands were on her chest, and she was staring straight ahead.

When the traffic light turned green, Yuniesky stepped on the gas.

"Don't worry," he said, and grabbed one of his mother's hands. "We should be at the hospital soon."

A Brief History of My Parent's Union

They meet on Saturday night at a party in San Salvador. They are introduced by one of my mother's older cousins. My father is skinny, with good posture, and all nose. He chews gum as he flirts with my mother. He's not attractive except for his dark eyes, but somehow she finds his awkwardness endearing. He tells her a story about traveling overseas to Madrid on official business for his family. (The truth is that he was drifting in Barcelona, aimless and without his father's money, because he'd been cut off; sleeping on park benches and inebriated all day. But he doesn't tell my mother that until after they're married.) She thinks the story is interesting but strange. Then my mother takes a sip of red wine straight from the bottle they sneaked out of the party. The wine tastes fruity and bitter. She smiles at him, and he kisses her in the courtyard below a cloudy, drizzling, purple sky and right next to a noisy street gutter.

They start dating and fool around a lot, but her brothers are always near. All five brothers don't like him because they know he's lazy. Despite her brother's feelings, my mother slowly realizes that there are more things she doesn't like about him than she does. After three months of dating, my mother decides on a break one night after seeing him drunk, chasing after a promiscuous girl at a party. She ends the relationship before leaving on vacation to Guatemala with her sister Gabriela. My father gets upset because he has no other girls on queue except for a prostitute named Christina, and he doesn't really want to marry a prostitute. When my mother arrives in Guatemala, she meets an older, well-off bachelor that is enamored with her at first sight. His name is Roberto and he's a medical student. Roberto takes her and Gabriela on a tour of Antigua Guatemala.

My maternal grandmother, who is on the side of my father because she thinks my mother is getting old and should marry soon, sends her an overnight letter asking her to return to El Salvador and reconsider. My mother ignores the letter and has a short romantic fling with Roberto. They go out every night to restaurants and clubs, and pretty soon she stops thinking about my father. My grandmother sends her a second more urgent letter telling her to hurry or my father will marry another. My mother decides to return home one cool, breezy afternoon after spying Roberto engaging in rough sex with a local indigenous girl on a small hill near his father's house. She hides behind a tall, Caribbean pine tree and watches them with the curiosity of a child visiting the tigers at the zoo. She is disappointed, but not at Roberto, for she realizes she wants to be the wild, dark-skinned girl under him. She does not see Roberto again.

When she returns to El Salvador, my father hires maria-chis to perform under her bedroom window. She never goes to the window but cowers under her bedsheet in the darkness, holding on to a doll my grandfather bought her during a business trip to New York City before he passed away. In a month, she and my father are back together, sitting next to each other on a couch at my grandmother's house. He chews gum like a camel and snatches her right hand roughly, asking her to marry him. She tells him that she wants to think about it, but she knows she has already said yes inside. She is convincing herself to marry my father by listening to a deviant voice that tells her that this is the right decision, it whispers in her ear saying things like, "he's an interesting man, perhaps not the best looking, but honest and interesting, with worldly experience and you are twenty-eight now, and nearing that certain age when there's no other choice except to settle down and put away those dreams about soulmates and all that romantic nonsense that poets and composers espouse." But there is another voice that she hears which is much softer, but also loud (if that makes any sense), telling her the opposite, but she shuts it away pretending not to hear.

They get married at an old cathedral in San Vicente, but only two of my uncles attend the ceremony. At the reception, her new husband gets too drunk partying with his friends. There are fireworks, there are toasts, there is a band, and there are guests representing the twelve richest families in El Salvador. And they laugh and celebrate and toast the new-lyweds as bombs explode in the mountains and gun battles rage near the US Embassy.

My grandmother buys them a house. They go on honey-moon to San Andres Island, Colombia. On their fourth day, they go to Johnny Cay off the northern coast of San Andres to dive. It's just the two of them on a small rented boat. She doesn't dive and stays on the boat waiting for him. My father is gone for at least ten minutes when two dirty looking men show up on a skiff, and seeing her by herself, ask her if she's a tourist. She acknowledges that she is a tourist, and that she's from El Salvador. The two men act shady like thieves. They are also ragged and their teeth are yellow. One of them, the taller one, stares at my mother for a little too long. Her heart pounds against her chest and she wants to look away, but she can't. The other man has his hand on the scabbard of his knife, and he begins to talk about a beautiful beach where the three of them can go; a beach that not many tourists know about. She tells the men thank you but her husband should be coming up soon, and they will be leaving the island shortly. The one man with the knife tells her that her husband is a very lucky man. My father comes up suddenly, and the men leave. Who were those men, my father asks, as he takes off his tank. She tells him that they were fishermen, that's all they were. At the end of the day, back at their hotel, as my father sleeps, my mother cries in the bathroom. Back then she thought she was crying because she was afraid of those men.

When they return from their honeymoon, she opens her own design boutique working from home. He doesn't work, but pretends to be interested in attending college. He spends a lot of time with his drunken friends riding motorcycles like a big child. Meanwhile, she gets pregnant and has a baby; my older brother Miguel. She gets pregnant again but has a miscarriage. She gets pregnant a third time and I am born. She gets pregnant one last time, but has another miscarriage.

He treats me and my brother like we were his friend's kids, but I don't remember any of this. After much pressure from my mother, he decides to go to college just to get her off his back. He also decides to take a correspondence course from Argentina to learn hypnotism. He has sex with the maid, forcing himself on her after a night of very heavy drinking and a failed private hypnotism session. My mother pretends not to hear it, just hoping we won't wake up. One day she tells my brother Miguel, who is six at the time, to point out a want ad for a bank teller position she saw in the newspaper to my father while he's watching television and having a beer. He gets really mad at this and yells at her. Why are you trying to use my son this way? he demands of her. Their argument gets heated, and he slaps her in the face right in front of me. And this I do remember, for it was the slap heard around the world. My mother screams at him, saying that we could use the money. He walks away to his "study," slamming the door behind him.

The Civil War finally begins, and she has a black eye that she tries to hide from her family with Jackie O sunglasses he bought for her on a trip to Mexico City. The following day while sitting upfront at a friend's fashion show, she has on the same black sunglasses, and when she crosses her legs while reading a big fashion magazine, she almost covers her face with it, but elevates her head instead, facing the models on the catwalk who reflect off her pitch-black lenses.

For three whole months there is relative peace, until my mother decides to take the entire family to Disney World in Orlando, Florida. My father begins to act strange upon hearing this and tells her he wants to go, but without the kids. They get into an argument that doesn't make any sense to her at all. He ends up staying home while my mom takes me and my brother to the Magic Kingdom. When we return from the trip, he serves her with divorce papers prepared by a crooked lawyer, letting her know that he's moving out because he can't live with her and her constant nagging. My mother gets really depressed, and with help from my uncles, she moves back in with my grandmother. Our house stays empty.

A year after they separate my father passes by my grandmother's house to visit us. He sits next to me and my brother in the living room sofa and I don't recognize him, but I'm happy to see him. He takes us to a skate park, and as he watches us play, he sits back on a bench, smoking a cigarette. We are disappearing right before his eyes and him before ours. The day ends and he drops us off back at my grandmother's. He'll be back next weekend he says. We kiss him at my mother's behest. He smells like Old Spice and citrus. We don't see him again. Their divorce is finalized in 1981, as the first major guerrilla offensive in northwestern El Salvador is underway.

This Modern Man Is Beat

This modern man, Habib bin Habib al Fulan, buzzes into the first pawnshop in Florida City with shoulders sunk down and a thousand-mile stare. He clutches an acoustic guitar by the body like a farmer holding a chicken.

He joins a line of people and waits.

More people buzz into the store.

When it's his turn, he gently places the string instrument on the counter for the pawnbroker to inspect.

And a good moment later:

"What kind of a name is that?" says pawnbroker #1, while rubbing a decal on the edge of the sound board.

"It's Arabic."

"What?"

"Middle Eastern."

"From where?"

"It's from the Middle East. My grandparents are from Palestine. But I was born in El Salvador."

"That's some mix you got there," says pawnbroker #1.

"I'm not Muslim. I'm Catholic."

"Really," says pawnbroker #1, smiling.

Habib looks down. The pawnbroker studies him up and down with a smirk.

"I can give you $850 for it."

"It's worth almost $1,500. I was hoping for at least $1,000. It's in really good condition. I've taken really good care of it. I lost the case, but other than that..."

"You lost the case?"

"Yes. It's a long story. I lost it when I moved."

"Let me have a little talk with my brother Joe."

Pawnbroker #1 takes Habib's guitar with him and goes over to a small office in the back where a man sits typing into a computer.

Habib waits patiently, looking at the guns in the glass cases and the other guitars that hang on the wall. He compares hunting knives.

"He says he ain't Muslim," says pawnbroker #1, laughing. "He's Catholic, he says."

The two pawnbrokers laugh. Habib forms an uneasy smile in their general direction.

After talking with his brother, pawnbroker #1 finally returns with the guitar, handing it back to Habib.

"The most I can give you is $875."

"Thank you," says Habib, as he takes back the guitar and leaves the store.

Habib walks to the store next door. The pawnbroker behind the counter of the second pawnshop is a tall, overweight man in a black Miami Heat T-shirt and a green hunting cap.

The store is not busy.

"Hello there," pawnbroker #2 says smiling. "How can I help you?"

Habib smiles and hands him the guitar.

Then a good moment later:

"So your mother is back there now?"

"Yes, she is."

"She must like it better, huh?"

"Yes, she got tired of America. Too much work, you know."

"When did she leave?"

"She left in 2002."

"Do you miss her?"

"Yes."

"Do you think you'll ever go back?"

"No, I don't think that's possible."

"But the country is in better shape? I mean they got peace now and all."

"Yes, she's at peace now."

"I don't know if you remember the movie *Salvador* directed by Oliver Stone?"

"Yes, I think so."

"That has got to be one of my favorite movies of all time. Everybody knows that was the movie that kept that whole mess down there from turning into Vietnam. God knows Ronald Reagan was getting ready to ship our boys off. I gotta tell you, Oliver Stone is a fucking maniac with his storytelling."

"That was a pretty good movie."

They both are silent for a moment.

Pawnbroker #2 glances at Habib's guitar again.

"I can only give you $500 for it."

"Let me think about it," says Habib and grabs his guitar.

"It was good talking with you, man."

"You too, I'll see ya," says Habib.

The third pawnshop is across the highway in a building in the shape of a flying saucer. The front of the building is littered with banners advertising special interest rates and discounts.

Habib immediately enters upon hearing the buzzer and hands the guitar to the first available pawnbroker who happens to be an older lady with white, puffy hair and a long-sleeved, buttoned-down American flag shirt.

"Well, what do we have here?" pawnbroker #3 says, inspecting the guitar curiously.

"It's a Gibson. Like brand new. Not a scratch."

Then a good moment later:

"And your father left your mother just like that?"

"Yes, he did."

"That is just plain mean. To have the gall to ask your mother for a divorce the moment you all arrive from a trip to Disney World that he didn't even want to go on, that takes some nerve."

She studies Habib's face, like exploring for any sign of emotion. She then puts her hand over his hand which had been leaning on the glass case.

"I'll tell you what though," pawnbroker #3 says, "the Lord is watching and the bad things we do come back to us. That's the rule. So pray for your father. Pray for him and forgive him."

"Thank you," says Habib, "I will."

They look at the guitar at the same time.

"I'm sorry but I can't give you more than $700 for it. I wouldn't be able to make a profit if I gave you more. Is there anything else you have?"

"This is all I have. My wife and I are about to get evicted from the motel down the street."

"I'm so sorry to hear that. I really wish I could help you, son. There is another pawnshop about a quarter mile from here. You could try them."

"Thank you anyway," says Habib as he grabs his guitar and leaves the store.

He crosses the street again, walking for about three blocks. The day is cloudy, hot, and extremely humid. The heat is exhausting. The street noise is deafening. Habib continues down a narrow side road off the main highway until he reaches the Black Seas Motel. He takes out his motel key from his pants pocket, leaves the "Do Not Disturb" notice hanging from the door knob, and unlocks the door and enters room Seven.

The curtains are drawn and there is a figure in the bed covered from head to toe in a white sheet. The window AC unit hums, working its lowest temperature, giving the room an unnatural chill.

He puts down the guitar on a table next to the bathroom and then sits down on the floor next to the bed, crossing his feet like a boy scout in front of a campfire.

The small figure in the bed does not move, but there is a limp hand that hangs from the side. The hand is pale, and it has fake purple press-on nails with little constellations on them.

"I'm gonna get the money," he says, addressing the figure in the bed. "I'm not worried. I just wanted to see how you were doing. I have leads, honey. I got good leads."

Habib rubs the shaggy brown carpet with the palm of his hands. At that moment, he doesn't look up at the bed, but it's like he is talking at it and not the figure in the bed.

"I hate you," he says.

It's a small, stuffy motel room, and the mild light from the gray day doesn't stand a chance against the thick, flowery curtain. The dying light that barely penetrates gives the room a dreariness that hangs in the cold center, right above the bed, and seems to swirl like a downward spiral with the intensity of existential arrows pointing at the obvious.

"Please say something. Are going to stay in bed all day? You don't believe me? That's okay, I was lying. I love you. I'm always gonna love you."

Habib gets up, grabs the guitar and leaves the room making sure the "Do Not Disturb" sign hangs visibly from the doorknob. He walks north on the main highway with the neck of the guitar over his shoulder, and when the cars honk he salutes them back with a shy wave and a strange frown. He continues for almost a mile until he finds the fourth pawnshop. The building is gray as the sky and it's empty inside.

He presses the buzzer, opens the door when it unlocks, and walks right up to pawnbroker #4 who is sweeping broken glass next to an empty display case.

"Good afternoon," pawnbroker #4 says, "I'll be right with you."

The Pawnbroker leans the broom next to a wall and goes behind the counter.

"I'd like to know what's the most I could get for this guitar," says Habib, and gives him the instrument.

"Let me take a look. You want to pawn it or sell it?

"I'd like to sell it."

As he holds the guitar, he looks it up on his computer.

"We don't sell too many acoustic guitars, but I have a regular who was looking for this exact Gibson model. I can give you $1000."

Habib smiles at pawnbroker #4.

Then a good moment later:

"Thank you. You don't know how bad I need this money. I was just twelve hours from me and my wife getting thrown out in the street."

"That sucks, man."

"I lost my job three months ago and my wife hasn't been able to work."

"You know what? I'm actually looking for someone to work the graveyard shift at one of my stores on the other side of town. Do you speak Spanish?"

"Yes, I'm fluent."

"Good, just take this application and pen and fill it out for me."

"Thank you."

"Let me get the cash for you."

Habib starts to fill out the application form. He puts down the motel for his address. Pawnbroker #4 returns with the money, counting it in front of Habib who has tears in his eyes.

"You okay?"

"Yes," Habib says, wiping his face with his hands. "My wife didn't think I could get the money."

Pawnbroker #4 looks at Habib carefully.

"Really?"

"She doesn't believe in me. People used to say to me, 'Habib what you doing with a girl like that?' And I didn't care what they say because I love her and it's my decision who I want to be with. But she was so drunk on that strawberry Cisco yesterday, getting real hysterical, accusing me of not being a real man, of not following the rules of the world, that I'm never gonna provide for her and that I will never be great. And that hurt when she said those things, it hurt even more than when she punched me in the face."

"She punched you?"

"She lives to fight. I got really angry, you know, and I choked her until her feet stopped kicking. So she's back at the motel pretending like she's dead. But that's just how she is."

Pawnbroker #4 looks at Habib carefully now, with a gaze that shifts from pity to fear.

Habib continues: "I've been through a lot. And right now, this is a new life. She can take it or leave it."

Pawnbroker #4 reaches slowly for a small, silver revolver under the counter.

Habib catches his own reflection unexpectedly in a mirror that hangs next to the shotguns. He recognizes it. It's the face of a hyena scavenging. The space between the two of them contracts, and time stops, and no one enters the store.

The Second Time We Tried to Escape Cuba

The second time we tried to escape the island we came up with a plan to obtain a skiff with an old, rusty engine in exchange for our extortion services. Extortion was something I had never done, but I understood the basic premise of it. The man who hired us, an Ernesto Iglesias from Camaguey, wanted us to extort his ex-wife by kidnapping her cockatoo, Lolo, who had been a gift from her French lover.

The plan was to snatch the pink bird with orange Mohawk in the middle of the night, and then Ernesto would instruct his cousin in Miami to call his ex-wife, telling her that if she didn't give him a very specific amount of money, which she would have to get from her rich, French boyfriend, the bird would be eliminated. My best friend Henry knew all the players involved except for the Frenchie who apparently traveled to Cuba three times a year.

The only problem I could foresee was that this cocka-too liked to talk, and it slept in the same room with the owner. The house was situated two towns away, closer to Havana, which meant our escape would have to be quick, for the closer we were to the capital the closer we were to Fidel. After that, we would have to get to the designated safe house (an old deserted ranch in the mountains), and the rest was basically lying low and waiting for instructions from Ernesto who had hired someone else to pick up the money for him.

I ended up telling my mother I was going on a little fishing excursion with Henry. So when I was home that day, I walked around the house pretending to be getting ready for the trip, gathering fishing poles and looking for my cooler. She was in the kitchen boiling some yuca our neighbor Rosita had brought us the day before. It had been an okay week for her. My sister was planning on visiting while I was away and she was bringing my nephew, the little half Jew.

"I'll probably be back Sunday night, Ma."

"What am I going to eat?"

"Just eat the entire yuca, dear mother."

"And what if I get sick of the yuca?"

"I'll bring fish for us when I get back. Don't worry."

And there I was sitting on our old, orange couch packing my father's old duffle bag, while watching her in the kitchen feeling a little bit sad like I always feel every time I leave my mother. I really didn't care about anyone or anything back then. I'm still not sure how I became so selfish or if I was just born that way. Sometimes I felt like I was pretending to be the good guy that stayed home to take care of his mother, but other times I felt just a huge weight of undefined guilt on my back everywhere I went, where people knew me to live with my mother. As I watched her move about her little kitchen, that she used to rule so masterfully in her better days, I remember thinking that we had somehow switched places like in those American movies where the parent and child switch bodies. I was sitting there afraid for my mother like she was a little kid I was leaving. How did this happen? And is it fair? I was obviously a bad parent.

I collected my bag and my rods and kissed her goodbye.

"Don't do too much work. Try to take it easy and relax some. Why don't you go visit Rosita?"

"There's is too much to do around the house. Rosita is too busy for me to be bothering her."

"Rosita said that you are welcomed anytime. I just don't want you to sit around the house by yourself. Go out. Go to Rosita's house. Go see Don Selsio."

"I'll be fine. If I want to leave the house, I will do it. But I like being home. I enjoy doing chores. Why should I go out if I don't like being out there?"

"Oh come on, Ma. Don't be like that. Everybody likes to go out for a little bit. You can't stay cooped up here all the time."

"Please tell Henry to give my regards to his mother."

"Okay, I will, but please promise me that you'll go out somewhere for a little bit."

"Maybe I will go out. Maybe I'll surprise you."

I gave her another kiss on the cheek and looked down at my lovely mother, with her white, silky hair, and the pale, dry skin from avoiding sunlight. She was my mother who had turned into my daughter, and then suddenly I remembered that I wasn't really going fishing, and I felt like a goddamn traitor.

I made sure to grab my dog-eared copy of *La conjura de los necios* right before leaving the house. It's an American novel about a fat guy who lives with his mother in New Orleans. He thinks he's smarter than everyone and looks down on everyone from the top of his intellectual perch. I didn't understand any of the philosophical references, but for a whole year, I went to the José Martí library every other month to read all the books that are mentioned by the main character, Ignatius J. Reilly, and things started making sense. On a surface level, like the main character, I hated and loved my mother with equal passion. I wanted something just like what happens to Ignatius' mother to happen to my mother, that by some ridiculous incident of life she begins to live for herself again and I become magically released from this heavy burden. When friends saw me with the book, I never bothered to explain it to them. There was one time, I was high and drunk with Henry, and I told him the story in the book and he understood it all, but we never talked about it again. How did this book find me? It happened right at the end of a long, toxic affair with a married woman. She had just kicked me out of her house, and as I was walking in the light rain with my head hanging low and both hands in my pockets like a homosexual, I saw it on the sidewalk in front of el Malecón. It was a bright maroon softcover published by Anagrama in Spain with a cartoon of a fat guy in winter clothes holding a hot dog in his left hand and when I opened it, I read the first words: "*Una gorra de caza verde apretó la parte superior del globo carnoso de una cabeza.*"

Nobody really goes too far from their house in Cuba. The doors are always open because it is too hot, but no one really goes anywhere. There was always the thought of too much work for so little pay, so people rather just drink and fuck their lives away, hoping and waiting for something to happen like a lonely European *yuma* falling from the sky or a family member making it out so they could get money every month from Europe or the USA and then continue drinking and fucking and maybe someday, if Our Lady of El Cobre was benevolent enough, they would escape the island too and have complete freedom to succeed or fail miserably on their own terms. Being away from Cuba was like being away from your ruthless, yet personable father.

This was most certainly the case with Ernesto Iglesias for his wife had met this unnamed French tourist at the hotel restaurant where she worked. Ernesto had given us way too much information regarding the situation, but kept the names from us thinking that if anyone was caught, he didn't want it to get back to him anyway. So Henry and I decided to refer to this French guy as Jean. His wife would just be the wife.

Jean was rich, or his mother had been rich before him, and left him everything when she died two years earlier. According to the way Ernesto told the story, which he got from eavesdropping on his adulterous wife, Jean's mother was overbearing and never let him wander too far from her because she was one of those mothers that never cut the umbilical cord. And this particular umbilical cord was partly made of money.

So when she died, he was like a child that had just been released from prison. He just went crazy with all this new freedom. He was forty-four, unmarried, and had never even really been with a woman according to the tale Ernesto was telling. Long story short he went down to Cuba after a friend mentioned the abundance of beautiful girls, which happens to be our second-best export after cigars. So Jean came down on vacation and fell in love with Ernesto's wife and promised her everything. They met at the hotel where he was staying and where she worked as a cleaning lady. According to the rumors, she noticed Jean watching her one lonely night and she decided right then and there to seduce him. Others said that it was Jean—naked—that jumped on her, forcing himself on her one night, and she even might have been genuinely upset about it until a coworker told her about how much the guest was worth.

So the clumsy affair began behind Ernesto's back despite, or because he was never a good husband to begin with. He had two other women on the side and a pen pal from Canada who he was putting all his bets on to get him out of the island. But since he was a Latin man, and had to be loyal to the tradition or else he wouldn't really be a Latin man but a sad imitation of one, in our presence as he retold the story, he turned angry, then somewhat sullen, inspiring a collection of twisted, erratic thoughts upon discovering his wife's infidelity. Yep, Enesto was a real *singao*.

When the so-called betrayal was uncovered, he went to his wife and beat her until he was detained by the police. The wife fled to her aunt's apartment outside Havana. Jean immediately wired her 5,000 euros so she could start the exit visa process. He then flew in from Paris, begging her to marry him, and bought her the talking cockatoo from a street vendor in the outskirts of Havana so she wouldn't feel too lonely when he had to fly back to France. The cockatoo was a sentimental gift, for she had owned a bird exactly like it that her father had given her when she was very little. He bought her the bird before leaving to NYC for Cancer treatment as a kind of compensation for leaving her with a mean, unloving aunt. The aunt was annoyed by the cockatoo, which somehow had learned to say *puta sucia* from the neighborhood kids who always teased her whenever she went to the market or

ran any errands. The insult, as the cockatoo spewed it without understanding, was partly true for the aunt was indeed
a prostitute and thief in Havana hunting for *yumas,* and her
current state at that time was of a plump, old woman shaped
somewhat like a rotund building.

So one day the *puta sucia* came home drunk from a very
long night of working the streets, making a commotion,
turning over chairs and tables while Ernesto's wife, who was
maybe eight at the time, tried to sleep. When the cockatoo
heard the racket, it began its rant against the aunt, saying
the words *"puta sucia"* repeatedly. The aunt was so angry and
intoxicated she knocked the cage down to the floor with
a baseball bat and started stomping on it as the cockatoo
screamed, *"Puta!"* Ernesto's wife jumped out of bed and tried
to stop her aunt, but she was shoved out of the way. Her crazy
aunt continued jumping on the cage until the cockatoo yelled
its last *"puta sucia"* before its tragic demise: *"pu-ta ... su ...
su..."* So no surprise, the girl was traumatized and the tale, as
she told it to Ernesto and any man she would open her heart
to, became a kind of myth in her life. And those lovers that
did not care to listen and pay attention to the story would
lose her. Ernesto did tell us that if all she ever really wanted
was a cockatoo, then she should have just told him, and then
he started crying and yelling about how husbands and wives
don't really know how to communicate and how he loves
her despite being with all these other women and that it no
longer matters because he would still try to get a little money
from that *come pinga* Jean with our help before he steals her
away from him forever, and then maybe he would marry his
Canadian pen pal and leave this God forsaken island like
me and Henry were planning to. I remember his face being

pale when he told us the story, like the shock of discovering that his wife loved another man was like witnessing a ghost, and he put his head down on his hands for a moment and then raised it like me and Henry were priests, and he said something like, Oh how I hate this country, how I hate it so much. And me and Henry felt the same way but didn't say anything.

Ernesto was released from jail shortly after Jean went back to Europe, but he refused to let his woman go due to pride, so when he found out she was staying back with the same aunt that had so marked her life, he came up with the seed of the plan to kidnap the bird; but he needed someone else to do it. The only thing of value he had was the skiff, so when he heard from some fool with a big mouth about Henry being on the market for one, he searched us out, talking about the "fair" trade and the *quid pro quo* like they say.

Did we feel bad about helping a *come pinga* like Ernesto Iglesias with such a bad reputation against women? Just a little bit. We cared more about getting out of the island than how other people lived their lives. It wasn't really our fault if he wanted to take as much money from his wife and her lover before she high tailed it out of Cuba. It's not like we were giving him the gun. We were just kidnapping a fucking bird.

The cockatoo and Ernesto's estranged wife slept in the living room. La tía *Puta sucia*, now somewhat of an invalid, slept in the bedroom. And if that wouldn't prove hard enough, the house was two doors down from the local neighborhood CDR office.

This new cockatoo was named Lola *dos* and she had a white head, red neck with a green coat, and the only words she could mimic was "*mi amor*" which Jean had taught her to say.

When Henry and I began to think too much about a plan, I told him that we needed to stop complicating things and just act. What we wanted was the cockatoo, so we would just barge in, unarmed of course with ski masks, and take the bird with cage and all. The only thing we needed to really plan was the escape route.

"What if the door is locked? How are we going to get into the house?"

"Doors are never locked in this island, Henry. Give me a break, man. If it's locked, we break it down. She's sleeping in the living room!"

"Okay, okay, but what about if she has a weapon?"

"Please man, she ain't going to have no weapon. We go in, take the cockatoo, and run. That's it."

We stole a couple ski masks that were the colors of the Iraqi flag. We figured they would suspect Al Qaeda terrorists or something and not two aspiring *balseros*.

The night of the kidnapping attempt we waited until one in the morning to make sure the neighbors were asleep and there would not be many people in the streets. I remember the night sky being cloudy, and the light of the moon illuminating the crime scene. I would have preferred to do it when the moon wasn't out, but we didn't have the luxury for Ernesto wanted his money as soon as possible, and we wanted the skiff to leave this shit of a country.

We put on our masks and went into the alley that was next to the house. "Are we going to check to see if the door is unlocked first?"

"Well, yes, that would make sense."

"Who's going first?"

"I'll go first."

I remember not being scared but thinking how ridiculous I felt with that mask on just to get our hands on a skiff to leave the island. This wasn't about the cockatoo or the French or even the rusty skiff.

This was about leaving, it was about freedom to fuck who you want to, eat all the food you want, work and make money wherever you want to, and to live totally free. The cockatoo was the least of my worries. All this was about leaving.

I stood in front of the door with Henry behind me. I turned the knob and it was unlocked, and when I opened it I could hear faint snoring. The living room was almost pitch-black, and a fan was humming. Despite the fan, the place still smelled like pee. I noticed a bulky figure under a bed sheet on the sofa that I positively identified as Ernesto's wife. She was out like a light, and she didn't look anything like I pictured her. I pictured a tall woman with big breasts.

But she was rather small, very petite with a slim body with nice curves that took me by surprise. She had blond hair, and she was pretty.

When Henry tapped me on the back, he pointed at an egg-shaped cage covered with a communist youth T-shirt hanging from a chain by the foot of the couch. I could hear the cockatoo clicking its beak; it would not go quietly. I looked at Henry and then looked at the cage. Henry pointed at me, and I nodded. I gave him a look that said, *Si mongo*, I'll be the one to grab the bird.

I held my breath and went over to the cage. I watched Ernesto's wife's calm face and then I looked at the cage. Henry looked at me with the universal head movement of "hurry up." When I put both my hands on the cage and as

I began to lift it to remove it from chain, the cockatoo said, "*Mi amor, mi amor, mi amor!*"

The sleeping estranged wife opened her eyes. Then we heard a noise coming down the hall, and it was *Puta sucia* and she was on crutches.

"What are you doing? Police! Police!"

I yanked the cage and took it off the hook as the cockatoo continued yelling *mi amor*.

"You better shut up or we'll kill you," yelled Henry at the old hag.

The estranged wife screamed. I had the cage, so I looked at Henry and ran for the door. But right before I could reach the door I tripped and fell right before the doorway; Ernesto's wife had got a hold of my right leg. The cage rolled down in front of me and right out of the house.

"Noooo," she screamed, getting up before me, stepping over me to go after the cage.

Henry froze. I yelled at Henry to grab the cage. As he went out the door, *la Puta sucia* threw him one of her crutches that flew by his head. I got up and shoved *Puta sucia* to the ground.

When I got outside, Henry was wrestling with Ernesto's wife trying to get the cage away from her but she wouldn't let go of it, like she was fighting for her baby. I went and grabbed her from the back and Henry finally got a hold of the cage, pulling it away from her, but it flung up in the air and then it went crashing down in the middle of the street, breaking into two pieces. At this time, the neighbor's lights came on and the bitch wife bit my hand, and I let go.

The bird, quite ruffled, was out crawling right in front of the cage saying, "*Mi amor, mi amor.*" Henry and I looked at each other. I rubbed my hand and I think it was bleeding.

Then Henry, without hesitating, and I guess trying to make up for his lack of quick action in the living room, dove in the most nonathletic manner towards the cockatoo. In that short disastrous dive an onlooker without knowing the context to this sad and funny scene would have no option but to march alongside Henry and his desire for freedom because he was really diving towards Miami. Yes, he was diving to Miami and freedom and I was proud of him.

But I guess you really have to fight for freedom, for when he landed with an empty thud the cockatoo was already airborne and halfway to the tallest palm tree in the neighborhood. Forget the bird, I said, and we both ran away in opposite directions amidst a forming neighborhood crowd, the *Puta sucia* and the estranged wife.

Ernesto disappeared once he found out about the sad outcome of our mission. He was afraid the kidnapping attempt would be traced back to him, so he went to stay with a relative on the southernmost part of the Island in a little town called Baracoa. The skiff was confiscated by a fisherman brother of his and that was that. His estranged wife married Jean and left the country. Before leaving, she hired some neighborhood boys to find the cockatoo, which didn't really stray too far from the neighborhood. The *Puta sucia* died broke and alone. We never heard from Ernesto again, but there was a rumor that was told to me by my good friend Sebastian saying that he did eventually get to Canada where he died in some kind of freak work accident at a construction site.

And as far as Henry and me, we made sure to really go fishing before heading back to town, and I brought my mother back the numerous fish I had promised her. She was happy but I could tell she sensed disappointment in my face.

The Meanest Thing You Ever Did Was Kiss Me

I

Habib bin Habib Al Fulan was born in El Salvador in 1976 and came to Miami with his mother and older sister in 1986. They watched Rocky IV on the flight to Florida. Back then, as a nine-year-old, he thought they were going on a family vacation to Disney World, but they ended up staying.

Lucia Oribe was born in Miami. Her father was Afro-Cuban and her mother was Salvadoran. At that time, she was working as a kindergarten teacher. Habib and Lucia met at a club in downtown Miami in early June of 2010.

He wasn't even supposed to go out that night. He was tired of clubs; he had survived them all and left them behind. He was going through a bar phase then. But his friend Juan was celebrating his birthday with another friend (Bob) and a married woman he was having an affair with. That woman's name Habib forgets.

The memory of that night is murky now, but he's confident about certain facts. He remembers buying tequila shots for the birthday boy. He remembers dancing. He remembers standing next to Bob, facing a small VIP area while Juan danced with the married woman. He remembers two girls in bright-colored club dresses sitting on a red sofa. Were they looking at Bob or Habib?

Habib couldn't tell. The boys looked at each other and then they looked at the girls. The girls smiled. The boys returned the smile. The shorter girl, the prettier one, had eyes like coffee beans, mischievous and engrossing.

That particular girl pointed at Habib with her index finger and then, turning the same finger upside down, commanded him to come over. Now in a situation like this, a man can do many things. Most men would walk over and introduce themselves. Better men would not be so quick to do that for it shows weakness. They'd lose the higher ground so to speak.

Habib was usually a disaster with women. At thirty-two years old, he had only had two girlfriends his entire life, and the rest were just deep longings that never turned into reality. Throughout all this, there was casual sex with strippers, bartenders, and lonely girls that kept him from drowning in self-pity and loneliness. So yes, under normal circumstances, Habib would have walked over to her like a lost boy looking for his mother in a department store, but there was a voice—a commanding voice—that said, "DON'T GO OVER THERE."

It may have been the voice of God.

"What?"

"DON'T GO OVER THERE."

"Don't go over there? Are you sure?"

"YES, I'M SURE, DON'T GO OVER THERE."

Bob looked at Habib like a Marine awaiting orders. Habib in turn did not break his gaze from the girl. Then the voice said: "TELL HER TO COME TO YOU."

Habib smiled, nodded, and motioned at the girl to come to him. She acquiesced. Her name was Lucia. He asked her if she was Dominican. Lucia said no, she was Salvadoran. Her mother was from El Salvador.

Habib immediately responded with a big welcoming smile. "*I'm* from El Salvador."

They talked for about twenty minutes. She was there for a bachelorette party. She didn't usually come to this club but decided to come out tonight. Habib asked her what she was drinking, and bought her a second round. They talked about their love for the Salvadoran national dish—*pupusas*. Lucia asked him what he did for a living. I'm a copy editor, he told her. Sounds cool, she said, I'm a teacher. Wow, a teacher, he said, I would have never guessed. She smiled. High school, he asked? No, she said, tiny tykes in kindergarten. The stories you must have, he said. I wouldn't even know where to start, she said, rolling her eyes in exaggeration and smiling big, wide, and pretty. After some time, to not keep her from her friends, he made sure to get her cell phone number before she went back to VIP. Habib tried not to look in her direction too often, but when he did, they both smiled.

When he got home, he decided not to text her until Monday night. For two weeks they texted back and forth and played phone tag until they went out on their first date. He got the impression that she was a social butterfly, a very busy girl. When they finally got a chance to go out, he had forgotten her face, but not how she made him feel. She wanted to go to a Hooters restaurant to get hot wings. He was not at all surprised at her suggestion.

He picked her up on a Sunday afternoon in Hialeah at her parent's house. Lucia was wearing blue sunglasses and a purple camisole. He pulled up in his small, yellow Japanese clown car, which made her smile when she entered the vehicle.

"This is a very interesting color, dear, very lemony."

"Thank you, it was specially ordered from Japan for an extra two grand."

"Really?"

"No. Yellow is my favorite color."

"Post-it-note yellow is your favorite color?"

"Yes, yellow is a happy color."

"Yay," she said, "a weirdo just like me. For a moment I was afraid this might be a boring date."

"Me, a weirdo? Ha ha ha—NO!"

She laughed like a chipmunk, and this gave Habib a warm feeling in his chest as he stepped on the gas.

At the restaurant she watched him closely as he devoured a dozen raw oysters.

"You really don't like oysters," he said, between slurps. "And you call yourself a Salvi?"

"Yep, sadly I'm not much of a seafood person. But please, dear, enjoy. Don't hold back on account of me."

"Oh, I won't."

She removed her sunglasses and put them inside her purse. She sat up, wiggled her little body, straightened her posture, and grabbed the pint of beer in front of her and sipped on the foam slowly. Habib sipped on his own beer and got a good, unencumbered look at Lucia. It confirmed his foggy memory. She did indeed have very pretty eyes. Due to the hot and humid south Florida weather, she wore her hair tied back in a muffin-shaped bun. Her friendliness reminded him of a friend that lived in New York City.

In that moment Habib consciously placed her in the Friend

Zone. For some reason, he didn't feel any attraction. She was pretty, but she seemed more like an interesting girl to just pal around with. His guard dropped and he relaxed, and feeling quite glad he didn't really need to impress her at all since he wasn't interested. Then he realized that he was being himself on a first date for the first time in a long time.

They shared the twenty hot wings with a pitcher of beer while discussing many topics like El Salvador, family, Miami, traveling, and life in general. She had very interesting things to say. Moments of silence were hardly uncomfortable. There were many fake and genuine smiles mixed together, trying to decide which way to go. It was almost like two blind people feeling each other out.

In one memorable instance, as they sat on that high-top table in the balcony of this particular Hooters restaurant, a noisy passenger jet pierced through the clouds and they both followed the craft with their eyes and ears.

As Lucia gazed at the jet's lovely trail, she asked him, "Do you think it's coming or going?"

"Hopefully, it's going far away from this place."

"Why do you say it *like* that, weirdo?"

"I guess I prefer other places."

"Are you serious? I love Miami."

"Of course you do. It's different for girls like you."

"Girls like me?"

"All the pretty girls in this town are spoiled with ladies' nights and all these thirsty dudes tripping over themselves to get to you."

"You hate ladies' nights?"

"No, I just dislike the people that attend ladies' night."

"All the people?"

"No, not all of them, but most people; Miamians are assholes. Please pardon my French. They say New Yorkers are rude—bullshit—New Yorkers are genuinely goodhearted people. I meet so many awesome New Yorkers just walking down the street by myself. Miami is like a giant strip club. Most of the women here are just good to look at."

"You sound bitter, weirdo."

"Me, bitter? Naaah … it's just reality."

"You just compared all the women in Miami to strippers."

"I compared the city of Miami to a strip club, not the actual people."

"Uh oh, someone is backpedaling—beep, beep."

Habib smiled, rubbing the thumb and index finger together in front of his face like if he was crushing a fly, "Maybe just a little … bitter."

"Just a little bit," she said mimicking his voice, squinting, followed by her big laugh that was deep, but still melodic to his ears.

Then they both got quiet for a moment before Habib said, "I guess I've had a different Miami experience."

"Let's just change the subject," she said.

A breeze hit them, and they both smiled at the same time.

"So, when was the last time you went to El Salvador?" he said.

"Last year. I have a lot of family. Stayed with my cousin Rita and ate a lot of *pupusas* and *tamales*. I gained about four pounds! Good times."

Sometimes Habib thinks about that first date, trying to pinpoint the exact moment he crossed into the land of no return. The only thing he's sure of is that it must have sneaked up on him like an iguana jumping out of a bush. That was his definition of love: a very green and large reptile that startles you as you hike a nice, quiet trail in the Everglades. And the Everglades, of course, is the wilderness of your heart.

"And what about you? When was the last time you went to El Salvador?"

"I haven't been down since I was nine. So, like twenty-five years."

"That's a long time. Any particular reason?"

"Recently, I haven't been too curious, I guess. But before that, I didn't have my papers in order."

"But you have family over there? Or are they all here?"

"No, I have a lot of cousins and uncles over there too."

"And your parents?"

"They're divorced. I don't really know my dad. Last time I saw him I was about three."

"So, he stayed in El Salvador?"

"Yes, he's over there."

"Does it bother you?"

"Not really. What about *your* parents?"

"They're still together."

"That's good. Do you ever ask them what their secret is?"

"No, I kind of try not to question it. I feel like I would be jinxing them. They're so cute though, especially my dad. He drives me to work in the morning."

"Yeah, you mentioned you don't drive anymore."

"I got into a bad wreck, and it left me traumatized. I wasn't hurt—thank God—but I came to the conclusion that cars and I don't mix."

"That's very interesting," he said, smiling at her.

"Are you making fun of me?"

"Not at all. Why would you say that?"

"The doofy smile on your face, weirdo."

"I wasn't laughing at you. I was remembering something."

"Go on," she said.

"It's dumb; just some nerd trivia. It's nothing."

"Lay it on me. I enjoy nerd trivia."

"O … K, well, the writer Ray Bradbury hated cars too. He hated them so much he never even got a license. He thought they were death traps. So, you're not alone."

"Okay," she said, laughing.

Habib laughed too. "But go on, so how do you get around? Do just have weirdos like me pick you up?"

"Yes, my weirdo friends drive. They don't mind picking me up."

"Must be nice," he said, smiling. "Do you give them gas money?"

"Yes, of course. And food and good company and we have fabulous, weirdo conversations like 'which cafeteria in Miami has the best *pan con bistec*' and 'what makes a Miamian a Miamian?'"

"That's good."

"I'm a very generous tipper," she said, gazing at his hands that were flat on the table.

"You are?"

"Yes siree, I am."

Habib rolled his eyes in exaggeration and they both said, "Weirdo," at the same time.

"Jinx," Habib said.

"Jinx," she said quickly, after trying to beat him to it.

They started laughing and Lucia snorted a little.

After dinner Lucia goaded him into an empty piano bar. They sat a table to the right of the stage and ordered dessert and martinis. As they sipped their drinks Lucia reminded Habib about the parking meter and gave him most of the change at the bottom of her purse.

He clearly remembers feeling joy walking briskly in the light rain to put quarters in the meter. He wasn't sure if it was the music, the alcohol, Lucia, or everything combined. When he returned to the bar, there was a man sitting next to her at the table. Habib sat on her other side.

The man was a piano player. He was effeminate, so Habib didn't get jealous, but at first Lucia seemed concerned that *he would* get jealous. Habib could tell by the "oh no" expression on her face, and her body language which seemed to be leaning away from the man. The guy was loud, flamboyant, and flirty, and after telling a few jokes he left to play the piano with another man.

Lucia requested Billy Joel. The piano duo began the set with "Piano Man," and then a second round of martinis arrived at the table accompanied by a big piece of warm apple pie for both of them to share. Despite the piano bar still being pretty empty, the alcohol and the good-time piano music seemed to place Habib and Lucia in some kind of impenetrable "GOOD TIME BUBBLE."

Then there were more martinis. More song requests. More alcohol. Then shots. Then dancing and finally kissing. Habib noticed her smile curl, and it was exactly like a cartoon lightbulb appearing above her head; and right after squeezing his hand, she went to make a song request, placing cash in the small jar on top of the piano and whispering the song in the musician's ear; and at that point, he looked at her outfit and the whole back of her and everything he could see from where he was sitting, and he still remembers to this day thinking that he couldn't believe she was there with him. How did I even land that? That's when he realized it: he was looking at the girl of his dreams. But back then, he ignored it.

They left hand in hand down the sidewalk in the summer August rain and back to his little yellow clown car where there was more kissing, and more embracing, and more butterflies springing forth from his stomach. He remembers her there in the passenger seat drunk and beautiful. There was a lot of making out, and rubbing and touching, and clothes were almost coming off, but Habib stopped himself because her kisses were getting sloppy. She was too drunk and he was already in love. He looked at her once more, and then he turned on the ignition and drove to a gas station where he bought a six-pack of Red Bull. He sat in the car drinking the energy drink as she slept in the passenger seat.

When he arrived at her house, he helped her to the front door. She was able to unlock the door, and before continuing through the threshold, she turned to him, gave him a quick kiss, and said, "Text me when you get home, weirdo." He helped her a little more, and she was off into her house. He closed the front door, making sure it was locked, and returned to his car.

Upon arriving home, he noticed that she had left her cell phone in his car. The next day, when he got to work, he sent her a friend request on Facebook with a message telling her he has her cell phone. She replied saying, "Thank you! What a crazy night! No more Baby Guinness shots for me." He told her he'll drop her phone off after work.

On the drive to her parent's house in Hialeah, he recalled anticipating a warm welcome, but when he arrived, she didn't even give him a kiss on the cheek. He was confused about her demeanor, but he gave her the cell phone and said goodbye. Despite that, they went out again sporadically, perhaps around eight times, and just like on their first outing, the same things happened every time: the flirting, the good rapport, the eating, the drinking, and the drunk make-out sessions at the end of the night. It became a pattern, and Habib—who was turning complacent—became trapped in a kind of dating loop that he enjoyed somewhat but couldn't seem to break out of. At that time, Habib was living with his mother and Lucia lived with her parents. Adding to that, his dating logistics were out of whack because he and Lucia lived forty-five minutes from each other and they never got more intimate than making out in his car.

The last time they went out, he took her to an Oscar Movie Marathon at the multiplex, but she had to leave early to help her friend plan a wedding. Then after that, Lucia just sort of disappeared or was just not around anymore, he couldn't really remember. Then Habib noticed that her Facebook status changed to "In a Relationship." So, whenever the subject came up, he became really good at pretending that he didn't care. But his very close friends knew he was posing.

"So, what happened with that girl you were dating?"

"Nothing, I don't think we were dating. Not sure what it was, just passing time."

"Did you fuck her at least?"

"No, I did not."

"Why not?"

"I don't know."

His own mother, on the other hand, did not directly ask him about the girl he had been going out with and never brought home. She circled around the subject like all good, intelligent deceptive mothers do.

"You're staying home tonight, Habibi?"

"Yes," he answered from his bedroom.

He was pretending to read, but he was really sulking, feeling sorry for himself like an asshole.

"Wow," she said, placing emphasis on the "o."

Then she too would be pretending to be cleaning, or actually cleaning, as TV is blaring in Spanish in the background with some *novela* or three-hour variety show with skimpy girls Habib could only dream of dating.

And when he stayed silent, then she would press him again:

"Habibi, what's wrong? You love to go out. Where are your friends?"

"I don't want to … go … out… Ma. I'm trying to read!"

The elephant was definitely in the room and Habib knew it. He was getting angrier because he did not want to talk about Lucia, even though he had mentioned her before to his mother as the "Salvadoran girl," but had dropped the subject after she began to ask about Lucia's last name and her family, trying to find out what kind of Salvi stock she came from.

"And what about the girl?"

There it was. She said it. She said the words he didn't want to hear. Habib was about to yell back to her, but he took a deep breath and closed his eyes.

"What girl?"

"You know what girl, the Salvadoran girl."

"I don't want to talk about it."

"Habibi, she didn't deserve you, my beautiful boy. She lost."

"What?" he said, placing the worn-out, green copy of Ulysses on his chest. "What did she say?"

"Habibi, you will meet the right girl. You will be happy."

He didn't say anything. He turned over on his stomach and sank his face into the pillow.

"Habibi."

"What?!"

He turned over again on his back, "What?!"

"Habibi, don't yell at me please."

He grabbed the book again and reread the page with Stephen Dedalus walking the pebbled streets of Dublin thinking about prostitutes, Shakespeare, and chamber maids.

"Habibi, do you want some strawberries?"

He didn't respond.

"Habibi, I am asking if you want strawberries."

"Yes," he said, quietly looking over at the page again.

"Habibi, are you listening, son?"

"Yes mother, I want strawberries."

"Do you want a lot or a little?"

"I don't want a lot."

"Okay," she said, and started washing the strawberries in the sink.

Then she said, right as she was putting the strawberries in a bowl, "Habibi, I love you."

"I love you too."

She brought him the strawberries in a green bowl with brown sugar sprinkled on top. He ate them on his bed, and after finishing the strawberries and the section he was reading in the book, he went to the living room and sat on the sofa to watch the models on the TV with his mother.

||

About two months later, Habib decided to visit his friend Lou in San Francisco. His friend was living near SF State in Parkmerced, in a two-bedroom apartment he once shared with his wife, who had left him to go back to Miami.

"Are you going to go after her?"

"I don't know. She's being irrational. We're making so much money here. She misses her family, but I told her if we hunker down for a couple of years we can save enough and go back with more money."

"What did she say when you told her that?"

"She said she hates it here and she can't wait. That it's her or San Francisco, and I need to make a choice."

"So, you made your choice?"

"Nope, just biding my time, biding my time. *She* needs to make the choice. I gotta put my foot down. I'm not chasing her. I am the man here. She needs to listen to me—I am her husband. She will soon realize the mistake she's making. You know how much money I make here? Nurses make six figures a year here just starting out. Think about that. Compared to Miami, please man, she'll come around."

They were sitting on the couch, with the television on but the sound off.

"How's it going with you and the chicks in Miami?"

"Not too good. I was sort of dating this Salvi girl, but she disappeared all of a sudden."

"Damn son, she sounds ice cold. Did you get any cooch at least?"

"Nothing. I really didn't have any place to take her."

"You should have taken her to one of those shitty motels on 8th Street. Or if you really needed to save the money, you should have just fucked her in the car—bust that nut and kick her out."

Lou was laughing now. Habib gave him an uneasy smile.

"I don't think she was that type of girl."

"Oh please, they're all like that man. You should have just whipped it out and here you go darling."

"It's complicated when you don't have your own place."

"That's sucks man. You really need to move out of your mom's house soon."

"Yeah, planning on it, it's just that she needs me now."

"I know brother, but what do they say? We're not getting any younger. You don't want to turn into one of those old, sad bachelors."

"I think about that. You don't think I think about that?"

"It's funny cause when I talk to my wife about you, she doesn't think you're ever going to leave your mother. And I tell her, well, that's all she has is Habib, but I'm counting on you, brother. I know you're going to do it and be happy. You gotta help yourself. I believe in you, my friend."

"Thank you," Habib said.

"But check it out. The girls here are not as hot as Miami chicks, but they are way friendlier and more approachable. We can go on the hunt tonight."

"Cool," Habib said, even though he didn't really feel like looking for anybody.

They went to a jazz festival in the day and then at night met up with a lively group of Lou's coworkers at a gay dive bar on Castro by the curious name of the West Coast Tool Box. Early in the evening it was empty, but then it picked up so much that the dance floor was crowded with men and women. Lou was talking to a co-worker of his, another nurse by the name of Amanda. She was divorced with two daughters.

"She's coming back, you watch."

"Do you love your wife?"

"Of course I do! What kind of question is that?"

"Then you should go after her. Listen to me Lou—"

"Forget it; she needs to give me just a little respect. Are you aware of how hard I've worked for that woman? What am I saying? You've seen me whining and crying about her all the time at work."

"Listen, Lou, listen to me."

He was nodding and sipping on his beer.

"I'm listening but I just don't think you're looking at it the way I see it. What about me, you know? I've sacrificed."

"Listen to me," she said, clasping his face with her one free hand. "Are you listening?"

"Yes."

"You're being a selfish asshole. There are two people in a marriage. If you continue being a jerk, she's not going to come back and you're going to end up alone."

He didn't say anything. He looked at Habib standing in front of them and smiled. Lou's co-worker had long blond hair and a bright smile; she didn't look at all like anybody's mother. She placed her hand on Lou's shoulder and squeezed, telling him she was going to the lady's room.

Lou came up to Habib quickly, holding his beer close to his chest. "How's it going, man? How do you like San Fran so far?"

"It's nice, man, I'm really digging it; can't wait until we hit the Golden Gate Bridge tomorrow."

"It's a beautiful view; you'll get to see all the goddamn fog going over the bay. Then I'll take you up to Sausalito and the Napa Valley for a little wine and cheese tasting. I know a retired nurse up there with a nice little vineyard—it's beautiful up there. She got two cute golden retrievers to meet you at the front and got this tight little group of Mexicans helping her make the most delicious wine you will ever taste. I guarantee it!"

Habib was now picturing the vineyard and the Golden Retrievers and the wine tasting and … Lucia sitting next to him on the park bench taking a bite of cheese and winking at him. He suddenly had a little smile on his face that quickly turned into a frown, which Lou noticed.

"What's wrong?"

"Nothing," he said, fake smiling.

"You look like you're about to cry."

"I'm good, I'm good."

"Okay, you sure? Let me get you another drink; you're looking kind of empty."

Lou quickly got him another beer from a cocktail waitress.

"But anyway, where was I? But anyway, then on Sunday I'll take you to Alcatraz. You're going to love it. It's a lot of fun but depressing as shit."

"That's a curious observation," Amanda interjected, upon arriving from the restroom.

Madonna's "Like a Prayer" began playing, and the entire club was singing along.

"I feel the same way about it," she said, looking at both of them.

"There she goes, busting my balls with that sarcasm," Lou said.

"Why are you being so defensive? I'm serious. Were you referring to the part in the tour when they talk about the inmates hearing the New Year's Eve celebrations across the Bay? Right?"

"Yeah, exactly! Imagine being so close to freedom you can

almost taste it across the bay—if that shit don't make you shed a tear, then your heartless!"

"Except for one thing though, they're criminals; they were paying their debt to society. Fuck those guys. You're a real pussy sometimes, Lou, you know that?"

Lou's mouth fell wide open, and then turning into a smile, he said, "You're such a bitch, you're lucky I love you, kid."

The Talking Heads song "This Must Be the Place" started playing.

Habib was checking out a cute girl standing by the bar, but then he saw she was with a guy who grabbed her by the arm and pulled her towards the dance floor. When he turned back to his group, he was shocked to see Lou and his co-worker Amanda making out like drunken kids in front of him. Once Lou noticed Habib's awkwardness, he stopped himself, and looking at his friend, made a zipper motion on his lips and went back to making out with Amanda.

After that they went to a piano bar, but it was really late so they were only able to get one round of drinks and make a couple of song requests. At the piano bar, he made a conscious effort to not think about Lucia or her second favorite Billy Joel song, "Vienna," which somebody in another group at the place requested. But as the melody reached his ears, Habib told himself, "Just keep drinking. Keep drinking. Billy Joel is a very popular artist." When that place closed, everyone ended up at a '50s-style diner, and then they all went home.

Back at Lou's apartment at the end of the night, a very tipsy Habib stared at his phone, rereading Lucia's last text messages to him.

Then he began a new text addressed to her:

"Hey! Just wanted to check in. Hope things are good."

As soon as he hit send, he immediately regretted it. Habib wasn't sure how long it would take for her to respond or even if she would. He put his hand over his face, realizing he was being a weirdo again.

Then a reply came. He was afraid to open it. His heart felt like it was about to pop out of his chest.

He grabbed the cell phone and read her response:

"Hi Mr., how the heck have you been? I'm good. Still mooching rides from friends… :)"

He didn't know what to say.

He started texting something then he deleted it and began the message again.

"I'm good! I'm in San Fran right now on vacation! Just spent a crazy night at a piano bar and thought of you."

"Awesome! I hope you requested our song!"

"Yep, sure did—a lot of good-time memories!"

"Aww, I hope you didn't have too many Baby Guinness shots, and you're home safe."

"Lol not too many only ten."

"Lol you're so funny."

"JK"

"Well, be safe over there, and take care of yourself. It was nice hearing from you."

Then without thinking he wrote: "I love you, Lucia."

There was no response for about a minute, and Habib felt like throwing up.

Then she wrote back.

"Please don't do this. You're drunk, dear. Put the phone down and go to sleep."

"I miss you."

"Go. To. Sleep. Weirdo. Please take care of yourself. Bye."

Habib read and reread the text. He wanted to write something else, but instead threw his phone to the ground and went to sleep.

Around noon Lou walked into his room.

"Wake up bro," he said, lightly shaking him.

"I'm up, I'm up," he said, sitting up and rubbing his eyes. "What's up?"

"I'm going to Miami to get Gina back."

Habib was still sleepy, but he opened his eyes wider.

"Cool, man, when are you going to go?"

"Today man, I'm getting the next flight out."

"Wait, today? But I don't leave until Tuesday."

"It's cool, you can crash here. I'll give you a spare key. "

"Are you sure? I mean if—"

"I hate to do this, my brother, but I love my wife. I have to at least try. I can't be without my wife. If I have to go back to Miami or travel back and forth, well so be it."

"No, you don't have to explain, man, I understand. I'm sure I'll find things to do. It's just a couple more days. Just go do what you have to do."

"Thanks, man. I'm really sorry, will definitely make it up to you. Love you brother!"

Habib knew that, more than likely, Lou would not make it up to him. Married friends had other gods to answer to.

The next two days Habib walked around San Francisco like a ghost. He enjoyed the ride to Alcatraz on the ferry but did find the prison depressing. The day was overcast and muggy and windy with light drops of rain.

After the prison tour, he decided to eat at a bar on Fisherman's Wharf. There was a mirror behind the bar, and he avoided his reflection.

The next day he mostly stayed in and watched television. His flight was early in the morning, and he wanted to be at the airport with plenty of time.

When he got back to Miami, Lou rang him up to tell him he was officially back with his wife.

"I had to beg and she wasn't having it. So, guess what I did?"

"I don't know, what did you do?"

"I threw a Hail Mary; I said can we at least have sex one more time? And bam! I'm back in, my brother!"

"That's awesome," Habib said.

III

A month after the San Francisco trip, his friend Montes rang Habib up to suggest that he go hiking in Mexico in his stead. The flight was departing in two months, and due to a family emergency, Montes would not be able to attend. Everything was paid for except the hotel.

"If you want to forget a woman, you go up the monolith. Listen to me Habib … it will open your Third Eye," Montes said to him. "A good, challenging hike will put things in perspective for you. *It is* such a different thing to do in life. If your body is not strong, the elevation will be the first downfall. If you pass that, then walking for eight hours at only thirty to forty percent of oxygen at night could kill you too, so many things could kill you."

Then there was a thick moment of silence between the two friends like there hadn't been in a long time.

"But," Montes said, "when you come down your vision will be clear—you will be self-aware. A spiritual awakening will uncurl from the physical, mental experiment with the self."

Habib didn't really pay attention to most of it but liked the idea of taking off once again. As opposed to hanging around in Miami still thinking about Lucia, any diversion was a welcomed activity. He did apologize to her about the drunk texting, but did not reach out to her further. Despite the fact that she didn't seem too bothered, and to avoid any further complications, he decided to delete her number from his cellphone, but left her as a friend on Facebook since he was now using less and less social media.

Montes continued trying to sell the trip: "And when you are very old, and close to the end of your journey, your death eyes will twinkle as you take your last breath, remembering the day you hiked the monolith.'

Habib was sold on the idea so fast his friend didn't have to say anything further to convince him. Montes let him borrow most of the equipment he would need. He commenced training by jogging nine miles a week and weightlifting on off days. He found a great deal on the plane ticket, and took a direct flight to Mexico and then a bus to a little town full of hotels and bars and restaurants with a monolith theme for the tourists. Once there, he hired a young professional guide, and they were on their way to base camp for a day of acclimatization. When finally confronted with the great monolith in the distance, and despite his now rapidly growing fear, he decided in that short private moment that he had to go through with it no matter what. "Fuck," he whispered, "what did I get myself into?"

The guide, who went by the name of Aureliano, said they would camp most of the day and leave at sundown. Habib was having trouble with his tent, and the guide went right up and helped him. He was a very good guide. Habib was embarrassed that he had already forgotten his name. He decided to talk to him once the campfire was started, while they ate their meager-looking dinners.

"*Cual es tu nombre?*" Habib said, with an apologetic tone.

"My name is Aureliano," he said, in almost perfect English.

"You speak English?"

"Yes, I graduated from NYU."

"Oh," Habib said, "But you are from here? I mean you're Mexican?"

"Yes, I am a Mexican that speaks English, and went to NYU, and after he graduated returned to the land of his birth."

"Wow, what did you study in New York?"

"I studied Architecture and Literature."

"That's cool, two very different fields," Habib said.

"Not really, not to Ayn Rand."

"Who's that?"

"She's just a writer I hate, and my wife enjoys."

"You're married?"

"Yep, you?"

"No, never been married."

"Well, don't fret, you're not missing much."

"How did you meet your wife?"

"We met on a blind date like a week before I left to attend NYU."

"You went on a blind date before you were going to leave Mexico?"

"Well, I did it as a favor to my friend, who wanted to be with my wife's best friend."

"And you guys just got together, and she waited for you to return? That's nice—"

"No, we actually got into an argument about the politics of a famous Colombian writer that we both admire, which led to a shouting match about Ayn Rand, who I believe to this day is a cultist."

"Wow, and you still managed to get her number?"

"You say 'wow' a lot."

"Oh, yeah, I guess I do."

"It's okay, wow man. But to get back to my Mexican 'When Harry Met Sally,' no, I did not get her number. But she did get on my nerves. We didn't talk again until I came back from NYC. We ran into each other at a bookstore, in the damn philosophy aisle, and both started laughing hysterically the second we saw each other."

Habib was listening intently, and upon noticing this, Aureliano continued his tale.

"We went to get coffee and spent the whole day together."

"What did you talk about?"

"More like, what did we not talk about? It was good, I needed that talk."

"What do you mean?"

"Well, when I went to NYU, I had this obsession to marry a gringa and bring her back with me, but that didn't work out. So, I had sex with like three gringas that whole time at the university. I was terrible with women. And English lit girls are supposed to be the easiest. But I remember one night, after having sex with this girl at a party, for some reason I was thinking about Ayn Rand and that fucking book 'Atlas Shrugged,' and that led to me to thinking about my future wife and her argument which I thought was total bullshit, which at that moment, I couldn't even recall the details of, and then—"

"And then what?"

"I started weeping very quietly next to this beautiful girl. I had no idea why. I guess I felt like a weird guy, laying there next to this hottie after just having some crazy sex, and I'm fantasizing about another girl that I barely even knew or ever even kissed, like if I lost something very valuable that I would never see again."

"Wow, what a story. But did you think about her again after that? Did you ask your friend if he'd run into her?"

"No, I didn't tell anybody, I just put my future wife to the back of my mind until that day that I ran into her at the bookstore."

"So, then you asked her out on another date?"

"No, because after spending all day together, we had sex that night, then the next week she moved in with me, and six months later she got pregnant and we got married. And now, we got three kids, and I work as a guide for extra money."

"That's a great story."

"So, what about you?"

Habib stayed silent for a little bit at that question.

"I was dating someone, but it didn't go anywhere."

"Oh, don't worry, you'll meet somebody else. It's kind of like when we hike the monolith—don't look back—you gotta keep looking ahead and down, of course. Relationships are overrated anyway."

"They are?"

"Yeah man. You know how much I wish I had even five minutes to myself when I get home from work? How I pray for a quiet house? I haven't been able to watch TV or read a book in peace and quiet in ages."

Habib was getting ready to tell Aureliano everything about Lucia to get his opinion, but instead he stayed quiet.

"Cheer up," Aureliano said, tapping him on the leg. "Out here, thoughts of the flesh and past loves will only get you killed. Out here, it's pure living without the first-world worries and comforts. This was the original plan my friend. Let's get some rest now before we head out."

Habib got excited for the monolith until he pictured Lucia hiking up a treacherous trail like a ghost wandering the valley. He tried to take a nap, but she wouldn't leave his brain. He was good now, he thought, he wasn't going to drunk dial her from Mexico. It was over and he was fine because in reality there was nothing really there.

At sundown they started early for the summit. Things were going well at first, but as the hike gradually turned harder, he kept on. This was a test, he told himself.

He tried not to complain to Aureliano, but it was now obvious that he underestimated the challenge: he was dehydrated, his feet were starting to callous, and he was getting cramps in his lower back. At a certain beat down point, nothing made sense to him. He remembered looking up at the sky and thinking this could be it. He could hardly breathe and was starting to feel dizzy. Then after barely reaching the summit right behind a group of outstanding Australians, his body gave up, dropping like a tower of Jenga blocks collapsing on itself. Aureliano took a good look at him like he was in the presence of a child acting out a dramatic fall in front of his parents. Habib eventually came down on a mule, being pulled by a very old man with a Charlie Chaplin mustache. When he returned to Miami, Montes was ecstatic at Habib's efforts on his first hike.

"Wow, brother, I am so proud of you," he said, hugging him at the airport.

Habib was laid out in bed for almost two weeks because of the painful calluses on the bottom of his feet. At home, when he was totally alone, he tried to forget the monolith. He was all fucked up now, he thought, but either way it was liberating. He tried to feel his "Third Eye" on his forehead. He kept his bedroom door closed, forcing his mother to knock when dinner was ready. She tried to leave him alone mostly, because she knew he was now deep in one of his doldrums that she couldn't understand even if she tried. Habib sometimes felt like he was suffocating; she had turned into a roommate that he didn't really care to run into. All his excuses for moving out were now null and void. He was coming to the conclusion after all this time that he and his mother both fed their insecurities from the same fountain of loneliness. They were holding on to each other, but it wasn't helping either of them.

IV

Towards the end of that year, he went on yet another trip to the Dominican Republic for two weeks with his friend Michael Suarez Jr. Michael was a New Jersey Cuban that was married to a Dominican hairstylist that couldn't leave the country due to her immigration status; she was still waiting for the Green Card to come through. So she sent her husband Michael to visit her family and since he didn't want to go by himself, he tried to convince Habib to go with him.

Habib didn't really have to be convinced for, as soon as his friend brought up the trip, he said yes once again without hesitation. His birthday was coming up too, and a trip to the Caribbean sounded like a nice gift to himself. They stayed with Michael's in-laws in a little town in the middle of the island. They hung out at gas stations that moonlight as bars called *bombas*. They went to strip clubs. They ate fresh seafood. They danced bachata with a lot of women. They threw a lot of parties—they did everything they were supposed to do. One night, he was thinking about the monolith, but he was drunk and his thoughts were erratic. In that fantasy, the monolith was black, and Habib, a tiny white ghost, almost a blemish.

On another night, they went to a *bomba* to drink and play pool. The waitress that was taking their order was as gorgeous as a famous Puerto Rican actress that Habib couldn't remember the name of. She was really friendly, and he ended up flirting with her the whole night. Then one of Michael's wife's nephews told him they could pay for the girl and take her back to a *cabaña*. The wife had two nephews who lived in the house where they were staying, and Michael referred to them as the cousins. They were always together, and they looked like twins.

"What do you mean 'pay for her'?" said Habib. The cousins explained to him that some girls do prostitution on the side for extra money; that it's no big deal. Habib at first said no, but he was drunk and, after considering it for a minute, he agreed. The girl winked at him after he said yes, and he felt a little heartache.

Michael, who looked after Habib like a little brother, said to him: "Make sure you use a rubber, brother."

The entire group of men drove to the *cabaña* located in the outskirts of the town. The girl gave them the address and directions on how to get there, with the promise that she would meet them there once she got off work. Michael was sitting in the back with one of the cousins as Habib sat in the front passenger seat with the second cousin. Both cousins were tall and lanky, with the same elaborate cornrows, and severe fashion sense made it hard to tell them both apart.

Upon arriving at the right location, they pulled into the parking area that was made up of a set of parking garages connected to each individual *cabaña*. They parked into one of the empty garages and told Habib to get out of the car and wait for the girl inside the *cabaña*.

"Just go in there?" asked Habib, pointing at the red door at the end of the garage.

"Yes, bro," Michael said, "time to get your dick wet."

Michael followed that with a joke in Spanish, and everyone inside the car started laughing except Habib, who was now getting out of the car.

Michael got in the front passenger seat and told him that they would be back in a couple of hours. The room was already paid for, he said, so have fun.

As Habib was about to turn to go into the *cabaña*, Michael called him once again.

"Wait, come here and take a hit of this fat joint to calm your nerves."

The cousin sitting in the passenger seat carefully lit the medium-sized joint for Habib and handed it to him. Habib took a big puff and started coughing.

"What the hell is in it? It smells like fucking bleach."

"Don't worry about it, "Michael said. "Take another hit, it will help you."

Habib took another puff and coughed some more before

he started waving his hands that he was good now. Michael and the cousins started laughing hysterically.

As he watched them pull out of the garage and speed down the parking lot, pumping bachata at full volume, Habib began to have second thoughts. Inside the room, it was awash in red light. After shutting the door behind him, he sat on the bed and waited. There was some kind of S&M porn playing on the television with men and women hanging from ceilings. Next to the bed, there was a nightstand with a menu, and next to the nightstand, by the wall, there was a hatch with a speaker next to it.

The door to the *cabaña* opened slowly, and the girl from the *bomba* arrived. She smiled as she sat next to Habib.

"Did you ask for anything to drink yet?"

"No," Habib said.

The girl grabbed the menu, and spoke into the speaker next to the hatch, and ordered beer and cigarettes.

"I didn't know," Habib said.

"You've never been to a *cabaña*?"

"No."

She undressed, and in the red light, her beauty had turned demonic. Habib began taking his shoes and pants off. He clearly remembers feeling dread, standing in front of this woman in fear like she was a serial killer.

"What's wrong, *amor*?"

"Nothing," Habib said, smiling.

"Then take off all your clothes. Let's do this, *amor*. I'm so hot for you."

Habib knew that was a lie.

She grabbed a condom from her purse and placed it on the bed in front of him. It was a local brand of condoms.

He then took off his underwear and was completely naked.

"Get on the bed," she said, "and try to relax."

He couldn't relax, but he did as he was told and awkwardly sat back on the bed naked. She began to rub his stomach in a circular motion. At first her touch felt good, but then it made him ticklish and he moved back and away from her, sitting up on the bed.

"What's wrong," she said.

Habib didn't say anything.

She looked at him, and he started laughing. At first, she smiled uneasily, but then her expression turned serious. Habib couldn't stop laughing, it was coming in waves. She got off the bed and started putting her clothes back on delicately and slowly, as if she was giving him enough time to stop laughing, but he didn't. His laughter was cascading off the walls like he was a hyena.

After making sure she had all her things, she left the room. Habib stayed on the bed, engulfed by the red light as the pornography continued playing on the television. Then the hatch opened, and a bucket of Presidente beers was pushed through. Habib also noticed the cigarettes she had asked for, and he decided to smoke a cigarette and drink a couple of beers before his friends came back.

When Habib's friends returned, they found him drunk and alone sleeping on the bed. Once they got him back to the car, he told them that it was some of the best sex he had ever had. She was worth every penny, he said, and he might go back for seconds. The group laughed at Habib the entire way back to the house.

Then on the day before their last day in the Dominican Republic, while tipsy on Brugal rum and crossing a busy intersection in Santo Domingo, he swore he saw Lucia walking down the sidewalk. At the same time his eyes were following this doppelganger, an electric current ignited in the center of his chest, causing him to stop in the middle of the road. Tires screeched, and people screamed, and our poor, dumb Habibi was suddenly bouncing off the hood of a small car. Now flat on his back and facing a blue, cloudy sky, Habib felt a warm liquid trickle down his forehead. His vision was foggy. He remembered thinking, "Is this it?"

A circle of faces gathered above him, suffocating him. He wanted to speak but he couldn't form the words. Then one face from the circle stood out. It was the girl who he thought was Lucia; she was looking down at him. It wasn't his Lucia—her teeth were like large accordion keys—but from the back, she looked like Lucia's twin.

He closed his eyes and then when he opened them, he was on a gurney in the back of an ambulance that seemed to be deliberately driving over every pothole in Santo Domingo. His friend Michael was next to him.

Michael didn't hesitate to say the obvious, "What the hell happened back there?"

"I thought I saw a girl I know—"

"What are you talking about?"

"She didn't mean anything to me," he said, sounding defeated, looking away.

"O ... K ... WEIRDO."

Habib spent an entire week in the hospital before he was released so he could fly back home. He had a minor concussion and four broken ribs. The doctors recommended bed rest as soon as he got back to Miami.

Once in Miami, the American doctors discovered a ruptured lung as well which would take weeks to heal. His mother was so distraught she called everyone in the family. Some friends came to visit him, and others texted him wishing a speedy recovery. As far as his job, he would be forced to use the rest of his vacation days.

With all this time bedridden at home, Habib spent it on his computer and the internet, and eventually back to Facebook where he noticed that Lucia had posted a happy birthday note on his page. At first, he was angry, and then he was sad, and ultimately, he became obsessively hopeful and decided to stalk her Facebook to see what she was up to. He saw photos of her at a wedding; she was wearing a purple dress like all the other bridesmaids. Habib wasn't a fan of the color, but she looked very good in it.

There were more photos of Lucia at parties, or at a club, or intimate family gatherings, and in each one of them she had that clever smirk. In each photo, she seemed to be the center of the happiness in the room. Her round face was always so affectionate with the cute crinkle at the corners of her eyes.

After going through most of her photo albums, Habib begrudgingly admitted that she looked effortlessly beautiful in every single image. He then looked at all the other things she posted like funny memes about Miami life, and YouTube recipes by Gordon Ramsey. And still not one sign of the boyfriend. Then Habib came across her "relationship status" which now said "single." He read and reread it and said it out loud slowly, stretching the vowels with his tongue—"S … I … N … G … L … E"—and let out a girlish laugh.

"What does it all even mean?" he said.

That bitch, he thought, and then at that exact moment, Lucia messaged him:

"Hello Mr."

He reread the message four times. Then he closed his eyes and let out a deep sigh.

When he opened his eyes, he wrote this:

"Hey, how are you? "

"I'm well, how are you? Just wanted to reach out and say hello."

"I'm good. Glad to hear you're good too. Every time a Billy Joel song comes on, you come to mind."

"Lol, ditto. I think that's a given for both lol... Did you hear he's coming to town? ;-)"

"The Piano Man is coming to town?

"Yes."

"No way."

"Yep, Mr. Long Island himself."

"When is it?"

"New Year's Eve."

"Wow Billy Joel live in living color—wanna go?"

"Great minds think alike; we should discuss this in person," she wrote back.

Habib responded, "Yes, definitely."

She was writing something else. He could see the bubbles:

"So, tell me Habibi, what else have you been up to? Inquiring minds want to know."

He felt a warm, more gentle current spreading over his chest not unlike when crossing that street in the Dominican Republic right before he was struck.

He started typing: "There's a lot to tell. Where do I even start?"

"The best way to tell a story is to start at the end. Then you go to the middle and double back."

"Just double back?"

"Yes sir, just double back."

"Okay," he said, smiling. "Here we go, I think the beginning was you."

100 Ways to Propose to a Married Woman

1. You must buy her a more expensive ring with a bigger diamond. Real shiny.

2. Try to tell her she's beautiful as much as you can and really mean it.

3. Don't ever judge her because you're not exactly St. Peter either.

4. Love her in every other way that you can't normally.

5. Cherish each moment because she just might never leave her husband.

6. When you talk to her, never look away.

7. Always remember that no matter what happens, her heart is just as delicate as yours.

8. If you don't kneel on one knee, the proposal will not count.

9. Don't ever assume that you're *the* one.

10. Remember her love ends whenever she goes back home to him at night.

11. You and he (her husband that is) are two sides of the same coin.

12. If her husband kills you before your proposal, just have no regrets about your love for her, just embrace that dark veil and go out like a champ.

13. Make sure you keep that promise about a house with a pool.

14. When you have your first child, and they grow up to ask you how you guys met, just tell them you met on Match.com.

15. Promise her that you will be the perfect husband even though there is no such thing.

16. After she says yes, and you get married, just stay away from social media altogether.

17. Always remember that you're not living in the 1800s and you're not in Salem, Massachusetts and the love of your life is not a witch. Just don't drown her with your love, because she'll resent you.

18. Remember as you ask for her hand in marriage that *real* love is not like in the movies. Actual true love is ugly and divine at the same time like a marathon runner throwing up at the finish line.

19. She loves you and she might love him too, but it's not the same love. Or could it be?

20. Love is weird so you might as well propose, and this is your Hail Mary pass.

21. As you look up at her, remember that she's the most beautiful girl in the world despite her lies and cheating and hypocrisy.

22. You weren't looking for this and it just found you and now that it's here, you must own it.

23. You claim to anyone that will listen that she's your Ava Gardner, but is she REALLY your Ava Gardner? Perhaps she's more like your Princess Diana and you're the bodyguard?

24. Everyone will call you an idiot, but double down on your love because if your *"I love yous"* were lies, then you're worse than her.

25. If she gets pregnant and claims it's definitely, positively NOT yours, it's probably yours.

26. Don't demand a blood test, because legally you have no rights. You blood child will be raised by him. Get used to it.

27. Falling in love with a married woman is like enjoying a slick, sporty rental that you can't afford under normal circumstances.

28. She doesn't love you more than her husband. She probably doesn't love her husband, she definitely doesn't love you. But go ahead; love her as much as you want.

29. No matter what happens, you will never forget her scent. It will remain ingrained on the insides of your nostrils.

30. The scent will be so strong for the rest of your life that you will have nightmares and fantasies (Daydreams!) about turning your nose inside out to scrub her out!

31. Make sure you play the Powerball for a whole year so you can win the jackpot. With that money, you will drive straight to Tiffany's and pick out the shiniest diamond you can find. And don't forget her ring number is 7.

32. If she says yes, and she divorces her husband to marry you, there will come a time when you're spooning her in bed (after many years of being together), and you will be jealous of her until you die, you will have thoughts and plans on how to entrap her like a bird in a cage just for yourself until you get sick of her. You will think about these things for a long time, and your chest will be in pain because you will never do anything about it. You hate her and you love her, but you cannot be without her.

33. Remember that she will always be the woman of your dreams no matter how badly she mistreats you. But the reality is that you're mistreating yourself. As a matter of fact, you probably hate yourself.

34. And if there's ever a good reason not to propose, well the best reason is that you're not really dealing with all the relationship bullshit. If you were smart, you'd

realize you're in the best position ever, but you're too dumb to see that and your heart is just gushing with all that superficial love.

35. You broke every rule from that "Side Nigga" video you found on YouTube.

36. Stay away from Facebook. Watching her post things with her husband will just destroy you.

37. On the weekends when you don't see her, remain mysterious, always.

38. Be an open book on Tuesdays and Thursdays, but be a heart full of secrets the rest of the days.

39. Try to make her breakfast at least three times a week.

40. Don't let your heart crack when she's sitting next to you on your futon, rubbing her big pregnant belly, and she says no when you ask her if you can feel the baby.

41. It probably is your baby because she's sitting next to you in your apartment, waiting for her hubby's flight to land so she can pick him up from the airport.

42. Assure her, honestly, and with genuine love, that she will not go to Jewish hell if she decides to return to you.

43. Go on Wikipedia to study up on Jewish culture in case she really does want you to convert.

44. Her white neck scratched by her cat is like a damaged Mona Lisa.

45. You are a weakling sinking into her; meanwhile she somehow turned into your god. Or you allowed her to be your god. Or you were godless looking for a god and then you got her. But she's not yours to pray to or her husband's; she doesn't belong to anyone, not even to God itself.

46. If the baby looks like her, she will more than likely pass it off as his. Sorry dude, but that's the reality. So pray to God.

47. You can go over an outline of your relationship a million times in your head, but you will still always get the same result—two irresponsible adults engaging in an irresponsible affair.

48. You are Gatsby. She is Daisy. What this means is that you are fully aware that she will not show up to your funeral. Are you okay with that?

49. If and when you win the Powerball and you ask her to marry you (keep in mind you're asking a married, pregnant woman for another commitment she might not be ready for): try to do a joke proposal just to see how it goes… Then after seeing her reaction—bam whip out the ring!

50. How many times are you going to look into her eyes for answers about the baby? It's either your baby, or it's not your baby.

51. If it is your baby, when she turns twenty-one someday, she will seek you out and you better have a good answer.

52. Don't cry because you have no right to cry.

53. Don't take it personal if you don't get invited to the baby shower since it's only supposed be women and it would be kind of awkward if she invited the baby's real father—TOO MUCH PREASSURE!

54. She's the most beautiful pregnant woman you've ever seen, and you need to tell her that every chance you get.

55. Bake her cookies in the morning, make her soup, for God's sake FEED HER, and make sure you use all organic ingredients because it could very well be your baby.

56. When you see her flirting (like she usually does) with other people, don't let it bother you, just ignore it.

57. Make sure you really practice your reaction like a professional actor when she confesses that it is your baby. DNA test says—you are the father!

58. Pray every night for her and a healthy baby, not an ounce of bitterness … let all that negative shit go. This is all love, love, love, and more love. Bite the bullet.

59. When the baby is born, don't assume one thing or another. It takes months for babies to physically develop the facial attributes of the parents. And even then, the baby can end up looking like a grandparent.

60. Are you the father? Is her husband the father? Who cares? Does it really matter? She's not with you.

61. DNA tests are $40–100 dollars at Walgreens pharmacy.

62. Did Frank Sinatra ever recognize Ronan Farrow?

63. Don't go see the baby once it's born, because you will break down in tears at first sight.

64. Does this baby, whether you're the father or not, mean the death knell to your "relationship"? Probably not.

65. Marriage will never be sacred; for it is based on ownership. Now love, LOVE is sacred.

66. So she probably does love you, but she's pragmatic and therefore will make decisions with her head as far as the baby's well-being is her only concern.

67. You don't make enough money to take care of a family by yourself.

68. Whatever you do, please don't get drunk and slide into her Instagram DMs with a cheesy, romantic love MEME.

69. Why did you do that? Now you're gonna get depressed at her response for her husband's sake: "I'm married and I have a daughter. That was an inappropriate message."

70. DON'T RESPOND!

71. YOU RESPONDED!

72. At least you apologized and blamed it on the alcohol.

Now leave her alone and run into a hole and hide and wallow.

73. I guess this is the real test—does she really love you?

74. Do not go to Jared to buy a Hail Mary engagement ring.

75. Your cat will continue to destroy the shower lining as you constantly worry about the same thing.

76. Don't be too hard on yourself, as long as you don't contact her until you have to see her at work, you will have a little spine still left. You're still not totally whooped by a married woman with a baby that might be yours.

77. Life is hard. Despite the emotional messiness of this particular situation, things could be way worse. Way worse.

78. Eventually, you will have to move on. You don't really want to pull a Jay Gatsby. Do you? Oh God, you're a fucking idiot.

79. What are even the odds that you could actually win the Powerball? And even if you win, are you just going to disappear for six months and come back driving a Mercedes Benz? "I can take care of you now, and that baby, that might be or might be not mine."

80. The real fucked up thing in all this is that you love her more than the baby. The baby doesn't even matter to you because it could very well NOT be your baby, and

you would still be there for her. Is that true love? Or are you dumb?

81. There was a moment in this fucked up relationship/ sex tryst/love affair/call it what you will, when you had the hand, but you gave it up willingly, why did you do that?

82. Because.

83. Because, why?

84. I thought that her actions were the actions of a desperate person, looking for a way out of a situation that she was not happy with. Like a child acting out, is how I saw it. I didn't think anybody that started an affair like we did would just double down on a failing marriage.

85. How did it start again?

86. Hooking up in the women's bathroom at a co-worker's wedding.

87. What!

88. And yet, you claim to not judge her for those actions. She will be faithful to you if she ever leaves her husband and marries you. Correct?

89. I'm not saying she wouldn't cheat on me, but I feel like it would be harder for her to be unfaithful to me. We actually like each other. I know she likes me, and the way I love her and I'm there for her.

90. The way you love her? You sound like such a pussy right now.

91. Look, she clearly doesn't love her husband, but I know for a fact that she doesn't even like him. For a marriage to last, you have to at the very least like the other person. A woman that cheats on the month of her second wedding anniversary clearly doesn't like her husband. If you like someone, it would be a little hard to cheat. Not saying that you wouldn't.

92. What if she does love him, but she's just a serial cheater? What if she would have left him for you and all of a sudden you turn into cheated husband 2.0?

93. That's a good question.

94. Are you really willing to suffer through the same thing as her current hubby? Didn't you mention before that you're both different sides of the same coin?

95. I don't want to suffer. I just want to be loved like the best moments of our affair, when there was no one else in the world except us.

96. But you will suffer, more than likely. No? Is that what you think love is? Suffering for someone that will not love you the same way back?

97. I don't really know what love is anymore. I don't want to suffer. I love her. I love her very much.

98. So you want to prove it by suffering? Do you love yourself? (I know, it's a cliché.)

99. I think I love myself.

100. No, you want to suffer.

Marchesa

Once in the summer of '08, the conjoined twins, Fawzy and Habib Delgado, got jumped at a strip club in Hallandale, Florida. They were making their way to a lap dance when they accidentally bumped into a drunken patron with a thick island accent. The drunk patron shoved the brothers into a bar stool.

The brothers, being the optimists they were, shoved the man back, yelling, "What the hell, man? What's the big idea?"

The drunk patron's friends, who were equally drunk, jumped in and the twins were beaten so savagely that Habib would need 14 stitches on his forehead and Fawzy sustained a busted lip and a minor concussion.

Fawzy and Habib shared one body with two legs, two heads, and three-and-a-half arms. When they walked, they wobbled from side to side. They were thirty-two years old, and since Fawzy controlled the right leg, and Habib the left leg, they had to undergo five years of intense physical therapy when they were kids to learn to walk on their own. As one can imagine, they never really had a chance. A bystander that saw the fight, and was an eyewitness to the brothers' valor and fearlessness, described them as two of the loveliest fools he had ever seen.

What the thugs didn't realize was that the twins were club regulars and had over a long period of time become the establishment's mascots. They were so loved by the club that they had a table that was usually reserved for them.

And that explained the huge brawl that ensued, spilling into the street, involving bouncers, thugs, and the Hallandale police department. The culprits were later banned from the club for life. The twins were rushed to the hospital, followed by a long caravan of exotic dancers from every corner of Latin America. The waiting room at the hospital resembled Bourbon Street during Mardi Gras.

The name of the dancer that Fawzy and Habib had intended to get a lap dance with was Marchesa. She was an English girl with blue eyes and a brilliant smile. Michelle was her real name and she was born in London in 1976. Her body was thin, and her skin had a bright pink hue that made her look like a shiny ghost whenever she made her rounds around the club. She was undeniably beautiful, but she didn't look like an exotic dancer. She looked more like a Hollywood actress in the tradition of Ingrid Bergman.

Fawzy and Habib were her best customers, and after almost three years of lap dances and vodka-fueled conversation, they couldn't find the courage to tell her how they really felt. Since a lap dance with Marchesa was their goal on the night of the brutal attack, she felt guilty and stayed with the brothers the entire time at the hospital.

Then during a brief moment of lucid insanity in their hospital room, the twins asked Marchesa out on a date. They tried to ask her on a friendly date, but the words came out in the wrong order and it sounded like they were asking her out on a date-date. The movie date was scheduled for the second Sunday after their release from the hospital.

A week after they were released, Fawzy and Habib were having trouble sleeping. They both had the same recurring dream about watching a horrible movie with Marchesa. The only difference was that in Fawzy's dream they were at a movie house, and in Habib's they were at a drive-in. Either way the movie in the dream was so bad and tasteless, that Marchesa would get up suddenly and leave the theater without a word. In both dreams the brothers would then run after her into the lobby, and out to the street where she would disappear into a puff of smoke that rose up to the night sky. And as they wandered into the same busy street, yelling out her name, they'd almost get run over by a truck being driven by an androgynous samurai with black bangs and dark, dreary circles under his eyes. The samurai, angry and incoherent, would then pull his truck to the side, and stepping out of the cab quickly, he'd jump, perform a somersault in midair, and then lunge at the brothers with a sword, slicing them in half.

The brothers would then wake up in a cold sweat, staying up the rest of the morning arguing about which movie to take her to. Horror? Action? Comedy? Drama? Independent? They were afraid that if they didn't pick the right movie, they would be throwing away an opportunity to have a woman in their lives.

By Thursday night, they were so tired and groggy from not getting any sleep they decided to call their old creative writing professor from community college, to talk about the curious situation they were in. The professor, a German American quadriplegic cinephile by the name of Merkel, told the brothers to meet him at the Denny's restaurant across the street from his studio loft in South Miami.

When Fawzy and Habib arrived, Merkel was already there, waiting for them at a table in the middle of the dining room with two chairs pushed aside to make room for his wheel-chair. He was drinking coffee and he wore a blue Nautica jacket with scruffy long hair, looking very much like The Dude from *The Big Lebowski*. Merkel's eyes were blue, like the pasty, fading blue off the Florida coast before a big storm strikes.

And there they sat, the teacher and his former students: three bachelors with eternity staring them in the face each morning when they woke up alone, and late at night when they went to bed alone. They were the hopeful, lovely, bright, and distorted subjects in a painting done by a master from another dimension—a master that could not exist in their world; a master that would have to invent them out of thin air.

As Merkel stroked a warm cup of black coffee as dark as the blackest hole in the universe, Fawzy and Habib sat across from him with a small, tiny glass of orange juice and an orange soda. They all ordered the Grand Slam Breakfast.

"I think a comedy is the best choice," said Fawzy.

"See what I mean," said Habib, looking at Merkel. "He thinks comedy is a safe bet. Most guys will choose a comedy. What if she doesn't like the same kind of humor you like? It could be a disaster. A horror film eliminates that possibility. If it's good horror, she will be scared and get excited and it will be easier for us to get into her panties."

"Is that really all you care about?" said Fawzy.

Merkel watched them with a mischievous smile, like he was watching a man at war with himself.

"Maybe the question you two should be asking is, what does she like? What kind of movies does she like? Do you know?"

"She reads novels," said Fawzy, looking despondent.

"What kind of novels?"

"She's into Dan Brown and Charles Willeford."

"She likes thrillers and crime fiction—she has good taste."

"Of course," said Habib. "She's a stripper that can't do no wrong."

"Why are you trying to be clever?" said Fawzy.

"Because who cares what she likes? We just want to have sex with her."

"What the hell are you talking about? This is serious. She could be the one."

"What do you mean, the one? She's a stripper for god's sake."

"Are you telling me you don't feel even a little bit of affection toward her? She treats us with respect, she looks at us like we are people and not freaks. How can you talk shit about her like that?"

The server brought the three Grand Slams. Merkel ate while the twins continued to argue. "I'm not talking to you for the rest of the night," said Fawzy.

"Whatever," said Habib. "I'll admit that she is nice. And I guess she is our friend, but you are such a fucking pussy."

"I don't wanna talk to you, please shut up."

"What's this girl's name," said Merkel.

"Her name is Marchesa," said Fawzy.

"No," said Habib. "That's her stripper name. Her real name is Michelle."

"But," said Fawzy, raising his voice, "she prefers to go by Marchesa."

"That's an interesting name for an exotic dancer," Merkel said, while pouring syrup on his pancakes.

"Why is that interesting?" said Fawzy.

"Yeah, why," said Habib, while playing with his straw.

"Marchesa, in Italian, is the title of a noblewoman. The wife of a Marchese is a Marchesa. Where is she from?"

"She's from London," said Fawzy.

"There was an eccentric Italian heiress by the name of Marchesa Luisa Casati."

Merkel then fixed himself to be more comfortable in his wheelchair by replacing his right foot on one of the pedals.

"The artist Augustus John painted a famous portrait of her with orange hair like a wildfire and deep, dark eyes and red lips with a mysterious grin like the Mona Lisa's. I think he slept with her too. He was one of her many lovers. Jack Kerouac saw the painting and was inspired to write some poems about it."

The twins did not say anything.

"My college sweetheart, Daisy Donovan, minored in Italian," said Merkel. "She was obsessed with the Marchesa."

He paused, carefully picked up his coffee with both hands, and took a long sip. The twins watched him closely. After putting the coffee down, he continued the story.

"When I went to the hospital after the accident, she stayed with me every day. But when the doctors told me that I'd never walk again, I started being real mean to her because I figured she would leave me eventually, so I thought I better dump her before she dumps me. The last I heard she stayed in upstate New York and married an architect."

"Do you regret it?" said Fawzy.

"Every day."

"Really?" said Habib.

"No," said Merkel.

Then Merkel gave the twins a big smile and continued eating his pancakes. He had known them for ten years and knew when he had them hooked. Merkel loved telling them stories.

"So how is the screenplay going, guys?" said Merkel.

"It's going," said Fawzy.

"Yeah right," said Habib. "He doesn't want to start rewriting yet. He'll get depressed about not having a woman, and then drag me from our computer to the strip joint to go watch the girls dance."

"So no headway with the second act?" said Merkel.

"He's still stuck in the first act. I can't do rewrites at a strip club."

"Shut up. That's the way I like to work. I write a first draft and then I let it simmer for a couple of weeks."

"It's been a year," said Habib.

"It doesn't matter. You can't rush it. Don't you know most rewriting is done in your head? Not on paper. It's what Ernest Hemingway used to do."

"Fuck Hemingway. He was a homophobe."

"Fuck Tyler Perry."

"Fuck you. Tyler Perry is a genius."

Then, suddenly, there was a silence among all three. The twins began eating their meals.

Sometime later after everyone was finished eating, and with their plates to the side, they continued their movie discussion.

"This is serious," said Fawzy. "If we choose the wrong movie, that's it. It's over. A real man chooses the right movie on a date like this. A bad choice can just ruin the whole night. Even if it's her choice. So maybe before watching a bad movie with us she'll think that we're special, but after a bad movie, she won't think about us in any way and that's the worst thing that can happen, worse than death. It will be a living death and you will be dead to this person."

There was silence all around.

"Why are you such a drama queen?" Habib said, while watching curious customers walk past their table.

"I am who I am. And I'm telling the truth."

"Maybe you guys should take her to an action movie or a science fiction movie. Those are usually foolproof. It's not too serious, but not a dumb comedy. It's sort of in the middle.

Maybe right alongside horror."

Nobody said anything for exactly a minute. "I want to marry her, Merkel."

"Fawzy you need to relax. You can't jump the gun with a girl like this."

"He is such a pansy," said Habib.

"What do you want, Habib?" said Merkel, smiling.

"I … want … sex. I don't care if she likes us or not, but is she willing to have sex with us.

That's what I tell this sucker over here, but he doesn't listen."

"Being single sucks," said Fawzy, abruptly. "I don't want to be single. I want to settle down."

"Even though we still haven't finished the screenplay?"

"To hell with the screenplay. I wanna fall in love."

"You are such a hypocrite," said Habib, laughing. "Whatever happened to 'first you get the money, then you get the power, and then you get the girl'?"

"To tell you the truth," Merkel said, interrupting Habib. "You're both right. Love is important, Fawzy, and sex matters, Habib. You both share the same heart and body, and like two gentleman scholars you must be fair and meet in the middle."

"What's the middle?" they both asked.

Merkel placed his elbows on the table, rested his chin on the knuckles of his hands, and thought about the question which lingered in the space between them. He closed his eyes, and the brothers waited, patiently studying his face. His breathing was normal, and the aura he gave off was soothing and friendly, like sitting on the side of a mountain with a Tibetan monk.

He opened his eyes and spoke.

"The middle is two bottles of a very good Amarone, a couple of nice, fat joints, an extra-large, New York City style pepperoni pizza, and Fellini's *La Dolce Vita* on DVD."

"Are you for real?" said Fawzy.

"I don't mess around when it comes to this stuff."

"Really?" said Habib.

"No," said Merkel.

Why Are You Afraid of Growing Old with Me?

Her husband died on Saturday night. I didn't want to talk to her but she caught me on the walkway to my mother's apartment, so I had no choice.

"How's Al?"

"He passed on Saturday."

"Pauline, I'm so sorry—"

I gave her a weak hug because she had a funky smell.

"He's not suffering anymore. He's in a better place."

She seemed fine. I wanted to cry. But I knew deep down that it wasn't anything personal because nowadays I cried for anything.

"They took him to the hospice on Thursday and he was throwing his arms at the paramedics and I didn't even get a chance to kiss him goodbye. It was on the doctor's orders because they knew I couldn't take care of him anymore."

"You had no choice, Pauline. You did everything you could."

"Habibi, did I tell you he pooped his pants on the last day, and I had to clean it up? It was such a mess."

"He's in a better place," I said, realizing that this conversation could go on for at least half an hour. I was so close to the door but didn't want to be rude. Besides, her husband just died. So, I made up my mind to let her talk almost as much as she wanted, but the second I notice the conversation was going round in circles like she's prone to do, I will start inching towards the door. Little by little I will drag my foot closer to an escape.

"Rosita from the association helped me with everything."

"That's good Pauline, I'm glad. I was a little worried."

She lowered her voice and said, "Everything."

"Everything?"

"Every single thing I needed to do but couldn't do because I was a mess, she helped me with. I had him cremated because that's what Al wanted. He always told me he didn't want his body in a casket so people can stare at him."

"So no funeral service?"

"Nope, nothing, none of that. And guess what, Habibi?"

"What?"

"Al paid for everything himself."

"Wow, how did he manage that?"

"I had no idea how I was going to pay, and you know how expensive dying is. So, on Monday I'm going through his things and I find a j-a-r filled with cash m-o-n-e-y."

"How much?"

"A lot. Al use to go to the casino twice a month; I would let him go. I didn't like going 'cause it gets so smoky there, and I'm allergic to smoke. So, he would go around two o'clock and sometimes he would come back with at least five hundred dollars."

"So, he was saving this whole time?"

"Yes, and guess what else?"

"Lay it on me."

"It was the exact amount I needed for everything."

"That's incredible."

"Ain't it?"

"I'm so glad you're doing good, Pauline."

This was my opportunity to make a break for my mother's, but the door opened and I was now in the middle of the two. Oh great. Now my mother was giving Pauline her condolences from her walker. My poor mother, how strong she remains. I had to endure their conversation for ten more minutes at least.

"Anything you need Pauline, you let us know, okay?" I said.

"Will do, Habibi."

"Yes, anything," my mother repeated.

I smiled and closed the door, or else it would go on and on and on.

"Poor Pauline," my mother said.

"Poor Al," I said.

"Thank God you cut her off, she would have talked your ear off; but poor woman. I will keep an eye on her."

"You need to keep an eye on each other," I said, then put her take out Chinese on the kitchen counter next to the oven.

"Are you staying?"

"Nah, I'm gonna meet up with Ray at Flannigan's. It's Friday ma, I'll see you tomorrow and Sunday for groceries"

"How's work? You seem stressed."

"Work is work. It is what it is. We've been pretty busy, but it's about to calm down by next week and I'll get to relax a little bit."

"Busy is good. I pray for you and that company every night."

"Thanks ma, look, I gotta get going, darling."

I kissed my mother on the forehead, and after making sure the door was locked behind me, I headed out to meet my buddy at Flanny's. On the twenty-minute drive, I did shed a tear for that poor bastard Al. He didn't look too good in the end. The week before they took him to the hospice, Pauline asked me to come and help her move him from his wheelchair to the couch where he liked to sleep. He wasn't all there. He couldn't talk and he was out of it, just slumped on the chair, with a urinary catheter attached to the bag on the side—it wasn't a pretty picture to say the least. Al was huge, a good six feet, and he weighed a ton. At this point in my mid-life, I had turned into a weakling due to lack of exercise. Pauline had his left side and I had his right side, but Al just slumped down more—he wasn't helping us any. I was getting impatient; the apartment was around eighty degrees and it smelled of piss, and I was sweating my balls off. We tried once more and still couldn't move him.

We decided to get a neighbor to help us. Pauline ended up asking a young, bulky looking kid who was probably not older than twenty, and with his help were able to move him into the couch. As we tried to lift him, Al tensed up his body like a statue, but it was too late. He was laying there now like a very old baby—the Benjamin Button from that Brad Pitt movie.

It was a depressing scene and I was very self-aware of it; the smell, the heat, and the humidity inside the apartment felt toxic to the spirit. Then Pauline had us lift the coffee table next to the couch so he wouldn't roll to the floor in the middle of the night. This was all so sad, so very fucking sad. I felt for her, I really did. She was a poor, lonely old lady that never had kids and hardly had anybody, so I tried to help once in a while.

Me and the kid said goodbye, and as I walked to my car that night I remembered thinking that it was probably going to be the last time I would see poor Al, who had moved to South Florida with the only wife he had ever had to work at the airport as a baggage handler while Pauline worked as a nurse at a local hospital. They left everything in Chicago: a nice house; close friends, and family to start over down south because of the better weather and cleaner air and palm trees, and cocaine cowboys, and Cuban refugees at the wild southern tip of the USA.

So, as I got closer to the bar in my Toyota Yaris, I said out loud, "We're all heading that way—what's so depressing about that?" Might as well drink and eat some delicious wings and ribs while you still can. No?

I saw my buddy Ray waiting for me, standing next to one of the fish tanks behind the hostess stand, and we got a table and I didn't mention any of this depressing tale. Then two pitchers later and a belly full of pork, I noticed she had sent me an email—the woman of my dreams, the love that enters and leaves my life at her own will, the woman that I would drop everything for, the one that had my heart completely—the fucking bitch Lucia.

What did she want? my drunken spirit asked. Oh yeah, she still had some little boyfriend that she had while still wanting to mess around with me. How many times did I have to declare my love while she ignored it to say that "she missed me, everything about me," but we could only be friends.

I confessed to Ray right then and there that I was recycling again when he noticed my change in demeanor.

"You don't need that girl, man. You need someone that's only going to love you, man!"

"You're right, you're right, she's just my—"

"You're what, man?"

"How can I say this?"

Our server arrived to take away some plates.

"How are you guys doing?"

The unstrung guitar feeling of my heart coincided with the simple, yet direct question, causing me to look at my buddy to acknowledge that we both wanted shots in order to take this little Friday night to another level. Shots might make me cry, reminiscing about this broad, but I'm a crier, just call me THE CRIER.

"You know what, Bethany—"

"It's Stephanie."

"I'm sorry."

"Geez, man," Ray said, laughing.

"Shots," I said, gazing longingly at Ray.

"You want shots?"

"Yes."

"Yes," Ray said, slamming his hand down on the table.

"We have free Fireball shots when you order dessert."

My face, my whole body cringed, and I looked over at Ray liked if we were a really boring, gay couple: "That's too much sugar, honey."

"Excuse me?"

"That is a lot of sugar," Ray said, looking back at me and then at Stephanie:

"Do you have anything that goes down smooth, but doesn't taste like candy," I said, not really looking at Stephanie. She was too cute; I didn't want to cry again.

The girl made a face, "How about Baby Guinness shots? Coffee Patron and Baileys? Always goes down smooth and you get that tequila kick at the end."

"Let's do it! Thank you, Stephanie!"

We both laughed and started picking at what was left of the fries. The first shot went down so well, and it really picked up my mood.

After the second shot, we went back to talking about the love of my life, my Sally, my woe of a tale.

"Bizarro 'When Harry Met Sally'—that's who we are!"

"Us?"

"No man, you and I are Angus and Malcolm."

We both did the air guitar.

"I'm talking about that girl."

"Oh yeah," Ray said, "Stay away from her!"

Stephanie brought a third round of shots with water.

We both looked at them for a moment. My eyes were getting wet, but I wasn't going to cry. I had cried on the way here. No more crying. I am so done with crying, and then I thought about the email she had sent me. Why did I love her? I didn't remember anymore. But how did I know I loved her? I had no idea? We'd never even had sex; all we did was make out. She made me laugh a lot and I found everything she ever did adorable: every mannerism, the sound of her raspy voice, her ugly little bony hands which I longed to hold in mine. But I guess if we would have worked it out and gotten married, I would have grown to hate those same mannerisms and cutesy things she did—right? Who the fuck knows, for I had never married. I wasn't really confident that the grass was actually greener on that side. Whenever I got lonely, I always thought about that, that no matter what position in life you are, like a lot of humans you're going to find something to bitch about.

We finished talking about her. I didn't bring her up again.

I didn't go into much detail either, even though out of all my buddies, Ray knew exactly how I felt about this girl. We were too tipsy now, so we called it a night. So lightweight in our old age—SAD! Oh well, but what can you do?

I got home to my apartment and my two cats, (residue from a previous affair to a married woman) to watch a little TV around two a.m. Then I went to bed and kept waking up due to acid reflux from all that damn beer and pork. It was Saturday morning and I tried forcing myself to try to sleep the entire morning, so I kept going back to bed. Had some Alka Seltzer and tried to focus on sleep until I slept for a couple of hours, and then got a call on my cell phone which I had left in the living room.

I always left the cell phone on in case there was an emergency with my mother, but I wasn't sure who was calling me at this time and looked at the name and it was her—my Sally. Calling me at 5:30 a.m. on a Saturday. For a minute, I thought about not picking up. She actually had done this before but the last time, I didn't pick up. This time, I felt like I should and finally get to the bottom of this obsession that we have with each other.

I picked up the call and she said: "Hello."

"Hi," I said.

"How are you? I'm sorry it all became a mess. I didn't know this is how you felt still. I thought you were over me; I thought we could be friends."

"If I would have gotten over you that fast, then it definitely wouldn't have been love. But I was in love with you. I'm still in love with you, and all you do is come in and out of my life, manipulating me."

She was now crying, quietly.

"Let's meet."

"Right now?"

"Yes, we need to talk in person and square all this away. I don't want you to hate me. Please Habibi."

"Where are you? Are you in Hollywood at your sister's?"

"No, my sister lives at my parent's now. We're all staying at my parent's in Hialeah. I'm helping her take care of the baby. I took a year off work."

"You're not teaching anymore?"

"It's just a year off until I figure out what I want to do."

My mind was blank for a minute or so and then realizing the dummy I was for her and had always been, and the entire decade I'd been waiting for her, I saw myself driving down there to pick her up.

"We don't have much time, Habibi."

"Okay, okay, text me the address again," I said then, switching the lights on in my place and watching my cats jump on the table to get fed.

"Do you have a pen?"

"Yes," I said, grabbing a scrap of paper and pen, and I wrote down the address.

"Hurry, okay?"

"Okay," I said, hanging up and feeling my head banging from the hangover.

I showered fast, fed the cats, and grabbed some old nun-chucks from under my bed just in case this was some kind of insane set up, since I was indeed going down to Miami; didn't want this little misadventure to turn into the latest "Florida Man" headline.

Driving down in my little yellow Toyota Yaris that I loved some much, I started contemplating the extent of my idiocy.

Was I born this way? It's Saturday morning, and I'm driving down to Hialeah to pick up a girl who's used me as her emotional crutch for at least a decade. When did we meet again? We met sometime in August of 2010 at some club in downtown Miami. She saw me across the club and pointing her little finger at me, asked me to come over to her. I was about to, but I didn't, I nodded and asked her to come to me instead, and she did.

That little moment led to a phone number, and an incredible first date, and then more dates with absolutely no sex. Then she ghosted me, and her Facebook status changed to "In a Relationship," and I got really sore about it. Then add to this, one of my nephews got sick and eventually passed away. Then she came back into my life because she was having problems with her boyfriend apparently, and like the fucking idiot moron that I am, I took her back. And this time, I wasn't living at home with my mom, so I really tried. I took her to see Elton John and even paid a ticket for her girlfriend. We also went to see Billy Joel together. And still nothing. She went back to the boyfriend.

Then I started an affair with a married woman I used to work with and tried to forget her. But she would contact me out of the blue sometimes. We even ended up meeting again in Miami Springs where we confessed our love for each other, and then the next day she went back to the boyfriend again and I went back to my affair. It was all so ridiculous. She's probably an alcoholic with some kind of issues, but they couldn't be daddy issues cause her parents were still together, so none of it made sense. And what excuse did I have? I was just a dumb, lonely, wannabe screenwriter trying to find someone to love me because, apparently, I did have many daddy issues. Oh, well, *que será, será* … now I'm on my way to see her again … like some kind of dumb heroin addict … but this one was addicted … to love that … wasn't there…

I used my phone maps to find her parent's house. I always get lost in Hialeah. The sun was rising now and this Saturday was going to be beautiful, but you could hardly tell by my hungover face. As I pulled up slowly in the yellow beast, I see her—ahoy there—and there … she … is now standing outside her parents' house just like on our first date eight years ago.

I unlock the door and she gets into the car, and we both start laughing uncontrollably.

"Where to?"

"Just drive. Anywhere. We don't have much time. The baby is going to get up soon and my sister is going to be home around eight."

"Okay, I guess we could go to Denny's or someplace like that."

"Let's go to Starbucks."

"Starbucks isn't open yet; it's six a.m."

"Then how about a bar? There's that pub in Miami Springs. They serve coffee at bars."

I looked at her like she was crazy and as she gave me the stare back. We both exploded in laughter.

"See," she said, "this is what I miss. I miss this."

"I miss it too, but you have a boyfriend and I'm in love with you."

She rolled her eyes, "I thought you were over me."

"Over you? How am I gonna be over you when you're like my great 'what may have been?' You're my 'what if.'"

"I'm you're 'what if'? Oh please."

"I'm sure that's how you think about me? I mean, don't you ever wonder that? Don't lie to me."

She didn't say anything.

"There she goes—silence speaks volumes. Have you ever heard of that?"

She smiled like a cartoon character, uneven but adorable.

"Just answer me this—"

"There's the pub," she said.

I pulled into the parking lot that was completely empty.

"Oh please," I said, "let's just go to Denny's and grab some breakfast."

She nodded and I drove the next street over to the great American diner.

Standing outside the parking lot watching her go before me, I started feeling that great feeling of anything is possible again. She looked beautiful even from the back. It was weird, she looked exactly the same. She was so my style. I wanted her so bad and she knew it, I was a total sucker for her, a kind of suckerfish, if you will.

My stomach was cramping as we walked in, and I immediately realized I would need to take a "deuce" in a little bit. Mental note, moron: No coffee for you yet. Just order OJ.

We got a booth and I sat across from her because I didn't want to be forward in anyway, I wanted to keep her guessing. I got the OJ and she got a coffee, and then we sat there looking at each other and broke out into laughter again. Then all the feelings came back because they had really not gone anywhere, they were just in hibernation like those goddamn hibernating bears. Looking into those eyes again made me thankful, and even if she wasn't mine right now, I belonged to her in some way and she knew it and I knew it and I was pretty much screwed like the first day we met.

I thought of Pauline and Al; would Lucia take care of me when I'm old and decrepit? Was this real love? It has to be some kind of love or something.

"What's on your mind?"

"Did I ever have a shot? Like was there a brief window when we could have been together?"

"Yes," she said.

"Really? I actually had a shot. So, what happened?"

"It's complicated. I was going to school when I met my boyfriend, and it just happened."

"What just happened? What about me?"

"It's complicated, Habibi."

"What's complicated?"

"Things got complicated."

"I don't understand you, yet you still reach out to me like what? Every two years?"

The waitress brought her coffee and my orange juice. She didn't add any sugar or cream but just took a big long sip and then, bringing the cup down in front of her, looked at my face. I looked at her eyes and she tried to avoid mine, but I could tell there was some kind of love inside them for me; it was undeniable. Sometimes you just know, and I knew that's what it was.

"I'm happy," she said, "He's so good to me."

"I didn't ask you if you were happy or how he treated you. I'm glad he treats you good. But we're, here, right? Right now after all this time, I'm sitting across from you, and you're looking at me with that adorable smile I love so much."

"Habib, stop, I need a friend, I'm happy."

"Keep telling yourself that, darling."

She shut up, shocked, and sat back still studying my face. Why am I like this? Am I addicted to longing and emotional pain? I hardly even knew her, but there was still some weird connection that we had. It was all inexplicable, but I could feel it in my bones: her love for me.

"We don't have much time," she said.

I didn't care. I was over it. I was hung over and I needed to take a shit and now we didn't have enough time—well, we never have enough time, honey. I love you, but we're always running out of time. Love is a really dumb thing if you think about it; people will avoid it like the plague because they're afraid of some truth that will be revealed about them. When you truly find the "right" person, it's not any of that Nicholas Sparks shit, it's quite simple: true love strips all the fake personality traits you invent because it reveals you to yourself. Think about it? Only when you're truly in love is when you don't care what your friends think. This is the person that you chose, and who has chosen you, and now you are two instead of one like a bizarre mirror of each other. And that's why when you meet a couple that fit, like two puzzle pieces that don't ever ask why they're together—and it's not sappy love shit because they fit so good it's like they have always been like that—there is no "why is she with him?"

Is she afraid that if she and I were to be one, that it would reveal something about herself, it would leave her vulnerable? Is she trying to convince herself that I'm the type of guy she could be with? Who the fuck knows? All I know is that I love her, and I wasn't really sure why.

"We're going to end up at the old folks home, you and I," I said.

I had her laughing now.

"You find that funny, huh? Is that when you're finally going to give me a chance?"

She snorted and laughed some more.

"Are you going to make me beg for it at the Century Village Retirement Community? Well you know what? If I have to wait that long, then I will. Totally fine with that. Just get ready, because I'm a have a lot of Cialis and I'm ready, darling, I'm so ready for that nasty, old people sex like in that 'Love in the Time of Cholera' cause those old folks, they know how to make love and you just get ready because at that age there aren't any more consequences."

She was laughing uncontrollably now, and I was happy once again. And that's how I knew that I was in love because I could just sit across from her and that was all the oxygen I needed from her, for everything else would be the cherry on top.

And that was that. I went to the bathroom and relieved myself, and we headed back to her place. About three blocks from her house, Billy Joel's 'You May Be Right' came on the radio like God was sending us a message. We both broke down in laughter at the same time; this was the song she always requested when we used to go to the piano bar in the Grove.

She was laughing in the passenger seat, and I was crying in the driver's seat. Not sure if she noticed the water coming out of my eyes, but she kept on swaying to the music and laughing and glowing and being the woman of my dreams.

Which all of this really just led to the real question, the only one that really mattered: if we had actually ended up together would she have wiped my ass at the age eighty-five?

Would I wipe her shit at eighty-five? I knew the answer to
that one for I would happily, with tenderness and affection
and all the nurtured love of a lifetime, wipe her ass clean and
change her diapers and clean her babble and feed her. Oh,
yes, I would, yes siree I would.

Habibi Baby, Are You Listening?

A man and a woman sat in a floating, spherical booth in the middle of the dining room of a pancake house. The woman is doing most of the talking. The man, who has a friendly face with a solemn expression, just listens. It is apparent from their demeanor that they are in anticipation of their food to arrive.

"I think," the woman begins, and then pauses as if looking for the right words, "nobody wants to die alone, and if you have the money and you can do something about it, there's nothing wrong with that. You shouldn't feel ashamed. It's the thing to do now. People want love, and this is just one of the many ways in our modern society that love has evolved. I truly believe this is part of our evolution. I just don't think that it's for me. But I'm totally okay with other people that want to do that. The only thing I don't like is, of course, that little contribution that I made without being asked. You stole my identity and it was legal and society is fine with that, but I'm not."

The man did not say anything. He looked at her. It seemed like he wanted to say something but instead of speaking, he nodded and then cringed in a kind of friendly grimace like he did not agree but that's okay.

The woman continued: "But I guess my biggest reason was

that I really had a lot of things going on, and that's really why I couldn't go to the wedding. But despite the bizarre, yet somewhat flattering situation you've placed me in, I wish you, and your robot gal, lots of happiness."

"Her name is Lucia. I know all this seems very weird, and it is, but please use her name when referring to her."

"Okay, I wish you and *Lucia*," she said, making air quotes, "lots of happiness."

"She's an AI clone and she cost me a lot of money, and she's a walking tribute to you and I'm sorry. I should have asked you."

"It's fine. You covered your bases as far as AI Law is concerned. You really thought this through, didn't you?"

"Yes, well, how could I not? She's worth 4.5 million. I wasn't going to spend all my money on an AI clone of you and not name her after you. I mean, I thought you would be happy. People have huge celebrations when they find out a clone of them will be brought into the world."

"I'm not most people, Habib."

"I know, I'm sorry, I meant—"

"I thought all those times that you said you were in love with me were because of my quirky personality and fierce individualism and how I reminded you of some old Netflix actress from the mid-2000s."

"That's not what I meant."

The food arrived. Blueberry pancakes for the man and French toast for the woman. The robot server, on hover board, also refilled their coffee.

They ate quietly for the first few minutes and then casually began to talk about friends they knew, eventually returning to the same topic at the beginning of their breakfast.

"I mean if this clone-of-me-robot-thing makes you happy, then I'm happy."

"I gotta tell you," said the man, sitting back in his booth, extending his right arm. "She's physically identical to you but, inside, nothing like you. I mean, she's likable and fun and she might even talk like you and use some of the same cute phrases that made me fall in love with you, but she isn't you. She's her own person."

"That's a relief," she said, sarcastically. "So she's got my face, boobs, and ass but none of my annoying traits? Is that how it works? Does she fart?"

The man smiled. "Yes, she farts, and it smells like cinnamon."

The woman laughed. "You need to get your money back; you do remember my farts smell like cumin? The engineers totally messed up your clone order."

They smiled at the same time, and it was as if the tension from earlier had lifted. His eyes crinkled at the edges watching her animated face recover from the laughter.

He leaned into the booth, grabbing and taking a sip from his coffee mug. He ran his finger on the lips of the mug, like he was getting ready to say something.

"Is there something else on your mind?" she said.

"Yes, there is."

"Well, don't you know it is rude to keep a lady waiting? What is it?"

"Lucia and I, well *my* Lucia and I, would really like to be parents."

There was silence. She looked at him with the puckered-up face of a mother getting ready to scold her child in public.

"You want my fucking eggs, don't you? You asshole."

"I mean it's a win-win."

"What do you mean a win-win? You want me to give you eggs so you can have kids with my clone. What kind of shit is that? You are such a shitty person, let me tell you!"

"You're not going to use them. You told me you didn't want kids."

"It doesn't matter what I said. When I say I don't want kids it also means I don't want no fucking clones of me having the kids I might have had."

"Well these are the kids that you were definitely never going to have with me. Doesn't 'Rick the Pilot' already have kids? How's it going with Rick now, by the way? You haven't mentioned him. Did he finally leave his wife?"

"You are being such a jerk."

"I'm the jerk, huh? The idiot that gets friend-zoned for twenty years is the jerk. Of course. But let me correct you, I'm the idiot, not the jerk. Or did you already forget what you told me ten years ago when we went on that cruise together? What was it you said, 'It's just sex, Habibi, but if we both aren't shacked up by forty, we should get married.' Remember that?"

She looked down at the table.

"Actually," he said, raising his finger, "there is one thing your clone has that you don't have—she has a heart, she has a fucking heart."

There were tears coming down her face.

As he watched her cry, he felt a knot in his chest. He looked down at the table and then at her hands, which were ugly and small and didn't seem to fit the rest of her. His gaze then went up her arms, chest, and finally landed at her pretty neck that glowed like a lone white marble column standing in some bright green field in Greece.

"Do you really think this is what I wanted, a clone? I did it because I thought that it would make you love me, okay? That you'd finally say to me, 'Wow, Habib is going to spend a million dollars for a clone of me. That's how much he adores me. That's how in love with me he is.' And maybe, just maybe, you'd say to yourself, 'So what if my feelings for him are not aligned. At least I have someone that loves me *that* much and would do anything for me.' That's the reason I did it. Because I thought you would stop me at the last minute, and look at me with those big, beautiful brown eyes, and say to me, 'No need to spend that money, Habib, I'm here. You got me. Let's go for it.'"

He was crying and could not continue.

"But I didn't," she said.

"No," he said, wiping his nose with a napkin. "You did not. My plan failed, and now I'm married to a clone of you."

She smiled under her teary eyes.

"I'm sorry for all the pain I've caused you, Habib. I'm beginning to realize, through many recent disastrous personal events, what a horrible person I was to myself and especially to you. I too have a reason that I wanted to meet with you today."

His heart in his chest was pounding now. She looked down at the table.

"I'm moving to Titan."

"What?"

"I need to start over."

"Leaving Earth," he said. "But nobody comes back from Titan."

"I know that. I've given this some serious thought, Habib."

"Are you going with Rick?"

"Rick has nothing to do with this. I gave Rick an ulti-
matum and he made his decision. I always wanted to go to
Titan, *Habibi*. You know that."

When she called him Habibi then he knew she was serious.
That word tugged at his heartstrings. She always said Habibi
when she wanted something from him. It was his weakness.
He found hope in that word. Hope that she would love him
back.

"I know, you mentioned Titan a lot. I didn't think you were
serious."

"It's time," she said with a teary smile, "I start acting like
a responsible adult."

"Responsible adults go to Titan?"

"Yes, I think so. At least that's what this responsible adult
is going to do."

"Don't go."

"You will always have me; what are you talking about?
You cloned me, Habibi. I will always be there. And there's
Interstellar Skype. We'll be able to talk all the time. Please
be happy for me, Habibi."

"I just think this is just too abrupt. Have you really thought
about it? I mean Rick is not the only guy in the galaxy. And
my Lucia, I mean, *cloned* Lucia is not you. She looks like you,
but she's not you. Please don't."

"What would you have me do, Habibi, waste my life on
this dying planet? I can't live here anymore. I need a change.
I've made too many mistakes. I want a fresh start."

"We can get married. I'll divorce your clone. We can start
over. I'll be a good husband. We don't have to have sex. I
won't be annoying, please you can't do this."

"You know that's financially impossible. You will need

another million dollars to divorce her and then to deport her to Cloneland. The bureaucracy alone wouldn't be worth the trouble."

"Please, please, I'm begging you."

"Habibi, look at me. Don't cry, baby. You're my best friend and you will always be my best friend. We went through a rough patch, but we're good now. Titan is far, but we'll talk every day. And anyways, I have a reason now to keep in touch, because…I will want to know…how our kids are doing."

"Our kids? You're giving me the eggs?"

"Yes, Habibi, you can have my eggs. I want you to be happy with Lucia. I know those clones are not perfect, but you can make it work. I will want lots of photos of those kids of ours. I want to see them grow; even from Titan we will still be connected."

He covered his face with his right hand, wiping his eyes.

"Habibi baby, are you listening? You're getting what you want, and I'm getting what I want."

He sat back, feeling now like he had just officially settled in life. He felt a disturbed relief. I can make this work, he thought to himself. He had to get serious now, he was about to start a family. It would be a non-traditional family, but a family nonetheless. His dreams, sans true love, were coming true in a way. His dreams of becoming a husband, a provider, a father—it was all about to happen. Let's be thankful, he thought to himself.

"Let's be thankful," she said, grabbing his hands across the table.

The Magically Disappearing Toothbrush

He seemed to arrive in New Jersey out of the blue and was much taller than her husband. You could even say that he was the exact opposite. He was also better looking than the husband, even if looks-wise he was a bit rough around the edges. To Luz, the nanny, Habib bin Habib had the shining yet warped presence of a starving artist in the last days of his roaming Bohemia. If one were able to imagine Pablo Picasso on the cusp of *Les Demoiselles d'Avignon,* add to that the physicality of a semi-retired soccer player, you could say that this was a complete man; and if she were much younger, she would be smitten and foolish and clumsy, but she was now an older woman with a son and a daughter almost the exact same age.

"Luz, I'd like to introduce you to Habib—we used to work together in Miami. He's visiting for a few days."

Habib greeted Luz in Spanish and realized he was Palestinian like her best friend in Barranquilla. There were many Arabs in South America who, like Jews, were escaping the ills of their lands in the early 1900s. They came with Turkish passports. Her best friend's grandmother would tell them stories, and she still remembered them to this day.

But what she recalled most clearly was the delicious food at her best friend's house, like stuffed grape leaves and shish barak soup.

Luz had only been the Schulman's nanny for about six months; that was the same amount of time they had been living in Jersey City, New Jersey. Before New Jersey, they had been living in Florida, and they sold their house because of the husband's job or something like that. Luz was getting used to their muddy stories and how most of the time they did not make sense at all, but it didn't matter. In a week, the mother would come and relieve Luz, and she would return to Colombia for six months because her work visa was up.

They seemed like a lovely family and an interesting couple—the Shulmans: Sofía and Ari Schulman, a new baby, with their cute daughter of one and a half, Olivia, and a dog and a cat all living together in a two bedroom, two bath apartment. She was nine months and ready to give birth. This was going to be her last week at work, and then unexpectedly, this man shows up.

"Wow, she's getting big," Habib said, looking at Olivia with his gentle, yet piercing brown eyes that were as big as hers.

"Your Tío is here, Olivia—Tío Habib," Sofía said.

The girl had been chasing the dog, which was so excited about the new visitor. Even the cat seemed to recognize the man.

Olivia looked up at him and her face broke into a smile, and then the man smiled and he kissed her on the forehead.

"How are you, Olivia? Your Tío is here to visit."

Luz knew it really was not her actual *tío* and was just a friend, or family friend. She was still trying to figure that out. The man looked at the child and the child looked at the man with a shy grin, and it felt to Luz like love at first sight.

They didn't have any food, so they fed the man leftover chicken and Colombian arepas with slices of white cheese. The man was gracious and ate all his food completely. Her husband, Ari, wouldn't arrive until almost eight o'clock from his job at a makeup manufacturer.

The man was friendly and warm, and even asked Luz from where in Colombia she hailed.

"I am from Barranquilla like Mrs. Sofía."

"I need to go to Colombia. I've never even been to South America."

"You need to go soon. And where are you from?"

"I'm from El Salvador. My family is Palestinian, that's why the name."

Sofía interjected with a big smile, "Or so he says."

Luz smiled, "Yes, I know many *palestinos* in Barranquilla."

Then the dog Coco started barking at the door.

"That must be Ari; Coco starts barking as soon as he hears the elevator down the hall."

Since the man had his back against the front door of the apartment, facing Luz and Mrs. Sofía, he had to turn his upper body towards the other man entering the apartment.

Ari said a quick understated "hello" that didn't seem to be directed at anyone in particular. He placed an Amazon package down next to some boxes beside the door and, after closing, made his way slowly towards the table.

The two women notified the baby in the seat that "Papa was home."

The man stood up and shook Ari's hand, saying, "It's been a long time. Good to see you."

"How are you?" Ari asked the man, before trailing off and walking past him towards the child.

"Who's Papa? Who's Papa?" he said, walking all the way around the dinner table to kiss the child.

The baby was happy but did not say the word "Papa" until after the man that was visiting sat down to watch the scene unfold before him with a very keen curiosity that Luz found very interesting. She felt tension in the space between all three; there was an unannounced discomfort in the beginning, like a standoff was about to begin for a poker game and everyone was bluffing. That's what it was, Luz was caught in the awkwardness that Mrs. Sofía seemed to pretend was normal, but she quickly realized and remembered that the husband always brought that awkwardness into every room, like someone that wanted to be liked.

Ari had a deli sandwich in his hand that he placed down on the table after kissing the child.

"Is this where I should sit?" he asked, motioning to the seat next to the visitor.

Mrs. Sofía stood up and grabbed the collection of toys and mail that was on the place mat and put them away. Ari sat down next to the man.

The child looked at the visitor, and the wife looked at the husband who looked at the visitor, as Luz watched them all.

"When did you fly in? Did you rent a car?"

"No," the man said, "I took a bus from LaGuardia to the office where we met up. I arrived around 2:30 p.m."

"So, you went to the office?"

"Yes, he did," the wife said.

"I suppose you know people at the office," he said, as he unwrapped the sandwich.

The man addressed his wife, "Sofía, they ordered food at work today from that deli I mentioned. Remember I mentioned it?"

She looked at the sandwich.

He took a bite, and after chewing and swallowing, he looked at the visitor, getting ready to ask more questions that seemed to be on the tip of his tongue. The visitor waited. The wife waited, and Luz felt like she was waiting too. The child continued to be enthralled by the visitor.

"So why are you here? Visiting friends?"

"Yes, visiting friends," the visitor said.

"You have friends in New Jersey?"

"Yes, I know a couple people in New Jersey. Also, I have a friend that lives in Washington Heights I'll try to meet up with."

"Washington Heights? Where is that? Is that upstate?"

"No, Washington Heights is uptown."

"Oh, okay."

The husband continued to eat and then looked up.

"So, I guess you're going to the baby shower at the office tomorrow?

"Yes," the wife said, "he's going to go. If you want to go. Not sure what your plans are."

"Sure, I'll pass by."

"How long are you here for?" the husband asked.

"Just three days. I leave Friday."

"You leave Friday? Wow, short trip. At what time is your flight on Friday?"

"It's in the evening, around 8:30 p.m. I think."

"Oh okay, you'll almost have two full days then."

"Ari, I was thinking I will take Habib to Hoboken on Friday."

"Oh yeah, you can take him to brunch. Friday she starts working from home, since the baby is due any minute."

"Yeah, that would be great," the visitor said.

"Any other plans tomorrow?"

"No, maybe I'll hit the baby shower or hang around in the Lower East Side, there's a bar down there that I used to frequent back in the day."

Then the husband and the visitor talked about the bar and how to get there. He showed the visitor, on his smartphone, which application to use so he wouldn't get lost in NYC. They then moved their conversation to the living room, and Luz assisted Mrs. Sofía in cleaning up and then getting the child ready for bed.

The husband served the visitor and himself whiskey, and they sat on the couch talking about work and whiskey, and the best ratio to make the perfect Johnny Walker with coke. Luz overheard everything from the kitchen. Mrs. Sofía would interject into their conversation from time to time until they finally finished all the cleaning up, and she joined them in the living room.

After Luz finished getting the baby ready for bed by getting her into her favorite dinosaur pajamas, she brought her out to say goodnight. The baby was very curious and coy with the visitor.

"Give your Tío a kiss," Mrs. Sofía said.

All three adults waited their turn to get a goodnight kiss from the baby.

The visitor stayed for about an hour more. The husband suggested a bar he could go to which was a few blocks away. He gave him directions. They said goodnight to the visitor, and he was off into the night. Luz went to bed after making sure the baby was fast asleep, and in her room as she was preparing herself, she heard Mrs. Sofía and her husband in a loud discussion that quickly dropped in volume upon, Luz was guessing, becoming aware that she could hear them. She turned off the light and Luz remembered in the morning that she had dreamed about her grandmother's house in Barranquilla. She was in the house with Mrs. Sofía's daughter, and the visitor was outside the house with his back to the house, and right at the moment that Luz and the baby stepped outside, the visitor turned around and Luz woke up.

The next day Mrs. Sofía left for work late. She was rushing about and barely had time to have breakfast with her daughter. The week was clearing up, for it had been raining since Monday. Luz could see the sun coming out now. She suddenly felt joy after recalling that this was her last week before she returned to Colombia. All this came about as a favor for Mrs. Sofía's mother who was coming back on Saturday to help her daughter before the new baby arrived which would be soon enough. Her due date was in September—Mrs. Sofía was on her ninth month, right at the end. She hadn't gained much weight, but Luz didn't feel like it was all that strange for the kind of petite figure she had. Of course, the beginning of her pregnancy was very touch and go due to a lot of work-related stress that Luz was only told about during certain special occasions when Mr. Ari wasn't around and Mrs. Sofía had no one to vent to.

That seemed to be the kind of relationship they had—she would vent, and he would complain and criticize her about her decisions. It was almost like they were siblings, and not husband and wife. Luz realized early upon arriving in New

Jersey to take the job that a lot of their stress also had to do with the abrupt way they had left Florida.

Apparently, she learned later, they had sold their house and packed all their belongings in as little time as under a month so they could move to New Jersey. Mrs. Sofía had to request a transfer for her job from the Florida office to NYC. Mr. Ari had apparently had enough of Florida living and wanted to get a new start. At least that's the story she'd been allowed to hear.

This temporary job was just for three months but had gone on into five, until her mother arrives this Saturday. The family was lovely and the New Jersey neighborhood over-looking the city was pretty, but Luz definitely wanted to be out before the winter started. This was not a normal favor that she had agreed to. It was sold to her as free room and board, with pay, until September, and this was really a good opportunity to get away for a little bit and travel to another part of the USA she had never been to.

Luz had already cleaned up the kitchen after breakfast and was now sitting with the toddler getting her hour of daily reading her mother wanted every day. She was a happy child, the very light of the apartment when you really thought about it. The toddler was the one that brought all the joy. She called every dog by the name of their family dog, and every cat was a meow. In an hour, Luz would take her to the park across the street to play for a bit, then they would come back for a nap, and after the nap it was lunch time. Then before she knew it, it was dinner time and Mrs. Sofía would be calling to say she would be getting home soon.

When they were at the park, and as Olivia swung on the swing, Mrs. Sofía called to let Luz know that she would probably be arriving later in the evening to show her friend from Florida, Mr. Habib, around the city. She told her she could make the rice and chicken for the baby, but that she would probably be bringing home food tonight from wherever place she would take Mr. Habib to eat, and would let her know then. Luz acquiesced.

At four o'clock, Mr. Ari called to ask about Olivia and, like previous times, to find out what his wife's instructions where, as if she hadn't told him. Luz didn't mind telling Mr. Ari what Mrs. Sofía had said, except when Mrs. Sofía strictly prohibited that, which happened from time to time.

"If Mr. Ari calls, please tell him I said I was working late. That's it. Don't say anything else. No mention that I was planning to go to the store to pick up the pink galoshes for Olivia at Jacadi, or the fabulous black coat from Bergdorf Goodman, or the adorable pearl earrings I saw in the window of that little boutique in SOHO, or that I was having a late meeting with a client, or that the work event ended at 8:45 p.m. and going to get a bite afterwards with co-workers. Do not say any of that because I will tell him later and he doesn't need to know."

Luz sometimes would get a little anxious knowing she was stuck in the middle of these two—a husband who wanted to know every little detail of his wife's day and a wife who liked to keep some things to herself. Those traits seemed to be the crack in their shaky relations, and of course, Luz never felt bad about always taking Mrs. Sofía's side because she was a woman, and no matter what, a woman, even with all her faults and missteps and irrationality, was always right—always.

Their sometimes-strained relations reminded Luz of that quote by that German philosopher about marriage; she couldn't remember the exact words, but it had something to do with friendship in marriage, how it was more important than love and it was so true because you should never marry a roommate, you should marry a friend. Mrs. Sofía and Mr. Ari appeared more like brother and sister than a married couple. Luz had noticed from the beginning that they were more like roommates than lovers. There was no tenderness, maybe that's what it was. The only reason that it was so obvious to Luz was because of her parents; God blesses their soul, they were so in love.

That night Mrs. Sofía arrived much later but still before her husband. Mr. Habib was with her and they had brought Indian food for everyone. The conversation didn't seem as clumsy or awkward as the night before. They had apparently eaten dinner there, and when Mr. Ari called, Mrs. Sofía decided to buy food to go so he wouldn't have to drive all the way from his job to meet them. All this was recounted quite gradually in front of Mr. Ari, who did not seem to even bat an eye.

It had been a rainy week and this night was no different. Even though Mr. Habib was staying in a room across the park, Mrs. Sofía offered him their couch to sleep on. He declined politely while staring out of the third-floor window, watching the drizzle tap the glass.

"I can let you borrow an umbrella," Mrs. Sofía offered.

"That could come in handy," he said.

After Luz put the baby in bed, they stayed up a little longer while the rain cleared up. Luz could overhear Mr. Ari talk about his new job for a Japanese company and the differences in culture. Mr. Habib was yawning by this time, and they called it a night, of course after he and Mrs. Sofía recounted everything they had done entire day.

When Mr. Habib finally left and they all went to bed, Luz started thinking about her parents. They were so very old now. Luz and her sister Anna took turns visiting them and helping them, but it was becoming too much. They didn't want to put them in a home, at least Luz was still fighting her sister about it. They both knew that once one of them passed, the other would follow. They were connected, and it seemed like they had always been since they found each other.

They met at an insurance office in Cartagena where they both worked. Their mother was married, and their father was not. They went on to have an almost ten-year affair that resulted in the birth of Luz—a secret their mother kept from their father because she did not believe in divorce. It's a funny thing to reach the age of ten with the knowledge that the man you thought was your father wasn't your father. Then Luz and her mother and her baby sister left to go live in a bigger house with bigger rooms and a sun-drenched patio, that upon first entering made her ten-year-old self welcome the actual man that was her father as her father. And what about Luz's stepfather? He had left Colombia and married an Italian woman, never to be seen again.

Luz's mother never tried to explain the betrayal; she always chalked it up to the unfortunate incident of finally, truly falling in love after getting married. She just knew that no matter what, she would be with Luz's father, for his conviction was only as great as the love he had for her. Then she would look at Luz while recounting her affair that led to true love, and say that love is the only thing that really matters and you will know when you encounter it.

The next day Mr. Habib arrived at the apartment around 10:00 a.m. Mrs. Sofía would take him for breakfast to her favorite bagel shop on Jersey Avenue, and then they would return to take the baby to the dentist. Mrs. Sofía still had to get ready, and Mr. Habib had arrived in time for the baby's breakfast.

Olivia's morning eyes grew big as they watched Mr. Habib while he made funny faces at her, mouthing out "I love you" and "wow" as she ate most of her food. Meanwhile, the dog and cat under the table by his feet paid attention to everything.

Olivia was wearing a little T-shirt that read "Mommy's Little Helper."

Luz watched the man and the child develop a language of winks, smiles, and nods.

"Do you have children?" Luz asked Mr. Habib.

"No," he said, "I have a cat though."

"A cat?" Luz said. "More independent than children."

"Yes," Mr. Habib said, laughing.

"And what is the cat's name?"

"Her name is Gigi; it's really her mother's cat."

"Whose mother?"

"Her," Mr. Habib said, pointing Olivia.

"Oh," Luz said, still not quite understanding.

But at that moment Mrs. Sofía came out of the restroom, ready to go. She was wearing blue overalls with white sneakers. Her hair was in a ponytail.

"Ready?" she said.

"Yes," he said, standing up.

Their plan was that Mrs. Sofía would take Mr. Habib for breakfast and a little tour of Jersey City, and upon their return, the whole group would take Olivia to her second dentist appointment in Hoboken. Mrs. Sofía loved the public transportation and wanted to show Mr. Habib as much as she could before he had to catch the bus to LaGuardia.

Olivia started crying when she realized her mother was leaving, so they had to pretend they weren't going. Luz grabbed her and took her to play with the toy computer, and in a flash the couple was gone.

Luz would now play with the child for a few hours, maybe take her to the park and then a short nap before lunch, and after that get her ready for the dentist appointment. Mrs. Sofía was planning to return around 1:30 p.m. with enough time to make the appointment at 3:00 p.m. All she had to do now was get the girl ready for the park. They went to her bedroom that was next to the baby's bathroom and picked out a pink and white dress and a pair of pink crock shoes. She carefully and most skillfully placed a pink bow on the child's head and was almost out the door when the video monitor made a noise, and a speaker came on: "Hello, it's Papa."

Olivia ran to the camera. Luz picked up the receiver to speak to the voice on the other end.

"Hi Luz, is my wife still there? She's not picking up her phone."

"Good morning, no she left about fifteen minutes ago. She's going to take Mr. Habib to the bagel shop."

"Oh yeah, okay, so they already left. At what time is the dentist appointment?"

"It's at 3:00 p.m."

"Okay, but after the appointment I will try to meet up with you guys. At what time did he say his flight was?"

Luz rolled her eyes and, in her head, responded, "Why don't you call your wife again?" but she took a deep breath as Olivia tried to speak into the camera again.

"I think Mr. Habib has to catch the bus by 4:00 p.m. so he can make his flight. I think that's what Mrs. Sofía said."

"That is what she said."

There was a very brief moment of silence. Luz was still standing by the door. The child was staring at her.

"And how is Olivia?"

"She's good. We are about to go to the park."

"Okay, give her a kiss from Papa. See you tonight. If you talk to my wife, please tell her to call me or pick up her phone."

"I will."

"Bye, honey. Kiss from Papa."

"Give Papa a kiss," Luz said, motioning to Olivia.

The call ended and they took the elevator down with the dog on a leash. The Park was across the street, and despite the sun being out, everything was wet from last night's rain. Olivia pushed a stroller with a baby on it.

Quiet days like this, so wrapped up in her thoughts, Luz sometimes tried to remember her stepfather, a man she lived with until the age of two and a half or so. She couldn't remember much about him except the house where they lived. It was a lonely house. His face, at least in her memories of him, was a blank face. It was the face of the jilted. Ever since she had learned of the real story of her parent's union, Luz would think how funny it is to fall in love for the first time in the most genuine way after you've been married and your whole life is set, and then true love comes out of nowhere to derail every stupid plan you followed on the path to what you thought was some kind of happiness or contentment.

Luz's mother never did lie about that. She never did love her husband and either she didn't want to realize it or she just lied to herself to pretend that every marriage comes with love, but that institution—if you examine it the way a scientist studies a butterfly or a tree or the earth or the moon—it never did have love in its purpose, design, nor execution. It seems like every poor idea comes from money or property or poorly executed real estate disputes.

It was time now to go back to the apartment for a short nap and lunch.

Luz watched Olivia get on the metal horse.

"Time to go," she said, picking her up and gently putting her down on her feet next to her baby carriage.

Olivia, recognizing the direction Luz was pointing, began to push the carriage full speed.

"Be careful now," she said, and motioning to the dog, "Come on, Coco."

The toddler stopped, a bit wobbly, but kept her balance and turned to watch the dog.

"Coco," she said, pointing at the dog. Another dog and its owner walked by; she pointed and said "Coco" again.

Once back at the apartment, Olivia slept for about half an hour. She couldn't let her take too long of a nap or she would not sleep through the night. When the toddler slept, Luz prepared her lunch of white rice with cut up chicken in a kind of orange sauce that was left over from the previous night.

Then Mrs. Sofía called to ask her if she needed anything, that they were going to pass by the Dollar Store near Jersey Avenue. Luz said to please bring more wipes and that they were out of treats for the dog. Then Mrs. Sofía asked about Olivia, and Luz told her she was taking a nap but soon would be up to have her lunch. She told Mrs. Sofía that her husband had called. Mrs. Sofía said thank you, that she had spoken to him and might meet them later. Then she said that they were on their way back to the apartment and would be there shortly.

By the time they arrived full of bags, Luz was already feeding Olivia her lunch. Mr. Habib had bought her a toy car at the Dollar Store but kept it to the side until the baby finished all her food. She watched the visitor with inquisitive eyes once again while still focusing on her delicious lunch.

Mrs. Sofía pretty much collapsed on the couch.

"We walked around for a lot, didn't we, Habibi?"

"Yes, it was a real tour of Jersey City; you didn't skimp out on anything." He watched Olivia eat her food. "Hmm, looks tasty," he said, making eye contact with the child.

Olivia pointed at the dog by his feet. "Coco," she said.

"Where is Coco, baby?" Mrs. Sofía said.

"Coco," she said, then carefully chewed her food.

"Finish your food, honey."

They sat on the living room sofa while Luz continued to feed Olivia.

"Can I use your restroom?" Mr. Habib said.

"Of course," Mrs. Sofía said. "Use this one, the first one right there."

Mrs. Sofía took off her shoes and went back to the kitchen. Olivia was on her last bites. She asked Luz how the rest of her day had been. Luz mentioned the plane and the dogs and how Olivia pointed at everything, asking her what they were. Or at least, it seemed like she was asking what they were.

"She's very talkative today," Luz said, giving the child the last bite.

"Wow," her mother said, "You ate all your food. You make Mama so happy. Yes, you do."

Mr. Habib came back from using the bathroom and offered to walk the dog until they were ready to leave for the dentist. They had about two hours until the appointment and, as Luz recalled, Coco had yet to do a number two.

"Yes, that would be great," Mrs. Sofía said. "Thank you! Coco misses you so much."

The dog got excited as soon as he noticed Mr. Habib pick up the leash, running around in circles. The Siamese cat tried to stay away. Olivia laughed from her chair.

After a good moment of trying to get the dog to calm down long enough so Mr. Habib could place the leash on him, he left the apartment and Mrs. Sofía then said she would take a short nap. She was reaching the very end of her pregnancy, and she took her napping seriously, especially when far from the critical eyes of her husband. Luz would always make sure to vouge for her. The nap and the dog walk took almost twenty-five minutes each.

When Mr. Habib came back with Coco, Luz was almost finished picking out the clothes for Olivia. Mrs. Sofía was waking up. Mr. Habib was sitting on the couch looking through his backpack so he would be ready to just catch the bus after the dentist and eating.

"Don't forget we have to brush her teeth," Mrs. Sofía reminded Luz.

She got Olivia dressed fairly quickly in one of her little dog shirts and white shorts. Brushing Olivia's teeth was a team effort. Luz would place her on a stand so she could see herself in the mirror, and while Luz held on to her, Mrs. Sofía gently brushed her teeth.

With Mrs. Sofía holding onto the child, Luz opened the medicine cabinet and the baby's toothbrush wasn't there.

"Where's the toothbrush?" Luz said out loud.

"It's not there?"

"I brushed her teeth this morning. I remember putting it back."

"Maybe you misplaced it?"

"No, I'm almost sure that I put it back."

"It's fine," Mrs. Sofía said, "I have another in the baby's bag. Let's hurry because we're already running a little late."

Luz went to grab the other toothbrush, and they brushed the child's teeth slowly and carefully. But Luz could still not get the toothbrush out of her head. A toothbrush doesn't just grow legs and walk out. Luz didn't want to swear on anything, but she could swear now that she had replaced the toothbrush this morning after brushing her teeth. Where else could it be? It has to be around here somewhere.

She stopped thinking about it and went to the living room to grab the carriage. They had the bags ready, and they were all set. Mr. Habib helped them as well. They had to catch the train to Hoboken, which was a short ten-minute walk from the apartment.

The day was sunny and windy with a temperature in the low seventies. In the parking lot, Mrs. Sofía stopped and asked Mr. Habib to tie her shoelace. "Look at me," she said, pointing at her pregnant belly, "I can't bend down."

Luz smiled as she watched them go back and forth, laughing, until finally Mr. Habib got on one knee, almost like he was proposing, and tied her shoelace.

"Aww, thank you," Mrs. Sofía said.

On the train ride, Mr. Habib and Olivia both looked out of the window with the same curiosity. The car was almost empty, and there was enough room for the carriage. Luz didn't think she was going to like New Jersey either, she thought to herself. But the neighborhood where they lived had an adorable charm in addition to its hefty price tag.

At the dentist, Mr. Habib stayed back in the waiting room with the baby carriage and the bag while Luz and Mrs. Sofía went in with Olivia. She did not cry as much as they thought she would. She opened her mouth wide as the pretty dentist examined all her teeth. When they finished and got back to the waiting area, the dentist thought Mr. Habib was her father and Mrs. Sofía, despite clearly hearing the mistake, did not correct her, and why would she? To Luz, this seemed like a good example of their connection.

After the dentist, the plan was to find a restaurant. Down in the street, Mrs. Sofía asked Mr. Habib what he was in the mood for.

"Let's go for Italian—how does that sound to you guys?"

"That sounds good," Mrs. Sofía said while punching Italian restaurants into her phone.

She found one fast, also a deli, a few blocks away. Luz enjoyed going to Hoboken. It was also a very expensive neighborhood, but it was exciting watching the sea of people walking about—the American way of rushing about that she admired but didn't want to ever really be a part of. Being a nanny was enough. Luz enjoyed traveling so much because she could always pretend to be someone else.

Luz took relief in the knowledge that her parents taught her to have no regrets. You have one life, her mother would say, and when you realize what the life you are supposed to live is—the real one, without lies and hypocrisy—it is very liberating and you hardly ever think about the other lives that you could have lived. Luz thinks that's why she never

got married. She was self-aware at an early age that she had
a wild spirit, and marriage would only make her unhappy.

The Italian deli where they decided to eat was in the corner
of a building with a small but charming patio next to the
sidewalk. Inside the deli, Luz noticed the photos of Italian
celebrities hanging all over the walls. They ordered one meat-
ball sub and two fried eggplant subs. When the food was
ready, Mr. Habib went to pick up the order.

Mr. Habib called and Mrs. Sofía spoke with him, explaining how the dentist appointment had gone and where they
were eating, and the time Mr. Habib had to catch his bus to
the airport. It seemed like he wanted to meet up, but Mrs.
Sofía said that there was not enough time, that as soon as they
finished eating, they would take Mr. Habib to the bus station.

Mr. Habib meanwhile made cute faces at Olivia who was
sitting on her stroller, eating a piece of fried eggplant. Her
eyes met Mr. Habib's eyes, exploring his face as he stretched
his smile and eyes, trying his very hardest to make her laugh.
At first, the toddler was transfixed at his clown expressions,
and then she screeched full of joy and laughed, talking to
herself and finally letting Luz put another piece of eggplant
in her mouth.

When Mrs. Sofía hung up the phone, she looked at Luz
and Mr. Habib, "She really likes the eggplant. Luz, you got
to remind me to make some at home."

The toddler and Mr. Habib continued their communica-
tion across the table with winks and gazes, and that's when
Luz saw an image of her own father floating above their
heads like a blow-up doll. His face was so very old, but beautiful, because it is the same face you share.

Luz knew then that he had passed. She felt it in her chest,

but she ignored it. She would finish her meal, and they would pay for the bill and take Mr. Habib to the bus stop so he could catch his bus, and they would get back home and she would play with the toddler, and then early in the evening before it was too late, she would call home.

They arrived at the bus stop right as the bus was pulling in. Mr. Habib checked his wallet to make sure he had the correct change. Passengers were boarding the bus fast. He didn't have time for a proper goodbye. With his gray backpack, he kissed Mrs. Sofía on the cheek and hugged Luz. It almost made her cry, thinking about her own father.

He then gave the child a gentle kiss on her forehead as she sat in her stroller, and he ran across the street to board the bus which would take him to catch another bus to LaGuardia, and back to Miami where he was from. The toddler pointed at the bus as it sped away. It was a pretty day. Luz wanted to cry because she knew she would never see her own father again. There is no love like your father's love, she thought. It's the love that makes you blossom, and if done correctly, it whisks you away into a future as a loving adult that reflects a father's love wherever you may go.

A Realistic Epilogue

Hurricane Alice: He was calling me on Friday, but I didn't pick up because I was on the boat with Miguel and my mother and Joey. I'm trying to relax, and I could wait to hear the whole story when I got back. So, I let Nick know, maybe he could touch base—for God's sake they live practically next to each other, and they should hang more.

Hurricane Alice's Mother Patty: I don't know what he's waiting for; he needs to get the toothbrush tested already. What if it goes away? Just borrow the money. I told Alice to let him borrow the money. I know it's 400 bucks, but it's peace-of-mind money—that's the actual name of the test, according to Alice.

Some huge balls he has to fly all the way to New Jersey to steal a toothbrush. My hats are off to that kid; God bless him. You can tell he loves her and this child that might or might not be his. If you ask me, I'll tell you it's totally his. I can tell, I have a good eye for that.

Miguel: I told him to ice her out, but did he listen to me? NOPE. Meanwhile Trampolina is feeding him all that bad advice in his head. I see how she is. But he's broke, so he's just going to have to wait to get the test. But what he needed to do was run the other way, but instead he got on a plane—that's the power of the cooch my friend, and she's Colombian too, forget about it!

Nick: I texted him because Alice said he called her and she was on the boat and she didn't feel like picking up. So, I sent him a quick text to see how he was doing. Nothing specific. I mean he never told anyone at the office he was going to New York. I found out through Alice that he went. Then I got a reply from him about five minutes later, and he pretty much texted me almost the whole story, at least the stuff that mattered. He was waiting for the bus to LaGuardia. Mission accomplished is what he texted me first, assuming I knew everything. Alice told him not to come back without a piece of hair or a thumb sucker or part of a nail—anything that could be tested for DNA—and he brings back a toothbrush. Kudos to him because I would have never thought of that in a million years. So, there you have it. We call her the Black Widow around here.

Hurricane Alice: You know what he told me, he said that he actually drank whiskey with that string bean husband of hers. He's such a twirp. I swear, a light wind can knock him over. Please. His dick must be so small. How she ended up with him, we'll never know; one of the great mysteries. If I had to guess, Black Widow is in it for the money. Of course, Suckerfish doesn't believe that. But he's a suckerfish, what does he know?

Miguel: I told him that she's a Trampolina just like Alice. They're both cut out of the same cloth. Give me a break. Women like this; you have to be a man—*un verdadero hombre,* bro. A woman like Sofía will chew you up and spit you out in a heartbeat and leave you spinning for the rest of your life. Women like this will destroy a lesser man. Trust me on that, Papo. Dummies end up homeless and broken because of women like this.

Nick: Now I'm thinking, maybe I should do a DNA test on my own kids. I mean, this whole situation has opened my eyes. I mean, Tara was cheating with a pizza server. I mean, part of me is joking, but sometimes I wonder what if they're not mine—I could save a lot of money. But to get back to Javi, I always had a feeling about Sofía. I remember she would flirt with me sometimes, and I wouldn't take the bait, but you could tell in her eyes she's no good. A Black Widow is what we call her—did I mention that already? And Alice laughs, but it's true. Javi should get a pay day loan or something and find out once and for all. Then again, she could end up going after him for money. Does he really want that? He really should just thank his lucky stars, because he dodged a bullet and run as far away from her as possible. But don't get me wrong, I would have probably done the same thing. I mean look at her with those eyes and that little body; I'm sure he had fun. She's a pretty girl, not out of this world but what are you going to do? The guy probably hadn't gotten laid in a while, and that there is the crux of the matter.

Hurricane Alice's Mother Patty: Let's see here, I was gracious enough to host Alice's little sales award ceremony party she likes to have for her people every year. So, it was me, Joey, Alice, Norton, Nick—by himself—Natalia with Gerard and Sofía (Black Widow) with her little husband. So, I got to meet the husband in person, and let me tell you everything Alice said was on point. Good Lord have mercy, how does a beautiful little girl like her end up with such an unremarkable man? I'm asking, how does that happen? Well, we all know how that happens—wink, wink. Joey talked to him most of the night because apparently he's also from Staten Island—something I wouldn't really tell people if you ask me. But that's just me. I had an open mind. I gave him a chance, but he was socially awkward; I mean he talked—he asked a lot of stupid questions. He wanted to know about the wine or something. I guess maybe he was kind of forcing it, but we're all family here, you know—there's no reason to be shy. I mean Joey is like the life of the party. But anyway, where was I? Yeah, so he mostly talked to Joey all night. But yeah, he's short, ugly, and boring. I mean what did she see in him? I told Alice after they left that maybe he has a big cock, you never know. Maybe he's different in private. It was funny though, she's there with her little husband, and she's pregnant and beautiful carrying another man's baby—at least more than likely, am I right?

Hurricane Alice: I didn't want that little dweeb to come. But what could I do? I would rather have the baby's real father come. Let me be fair, he wasn't that bad, but he would just say stupid shit, like asking me about the grape and the wine or some shit. I tried so hard not to give him a look or any type of eye roll. I behaved, but in my head I was like, What the hell are you saying? You fucking dweeb. He's just so drab. He ended up talking to Joey all night because they're both from Staten Island. Let me ask you, who in their right mind is proud to be from Staten Island? Nobody. Staten Island Jews are the worst, ask anybody! Nothing funnier than two Staten Island Jews yakking it up. Yack it up—you fucking loser. Not Joey, just the dweeb.

Joey: To me, I didn't think he was bad. He was born in Staten Island and anybody from that god forsaken place deserves forgiveness, let me tell you. But he seemed nice. Was he a little boring? Yes. Do they fit as a couple? No. Is the baby in the oven his? Now that I meet him in person, I can definitely say that it is not his. There's no way he impregnated her. He has the vocal inflection of a limp dick, and please forgive me for saying this, but despite that I found him personable. We talked about my father's bar on Jackson Street. He grew up near there. I thought he was alright, you know, I didn't see anything wrong. Do they match? No, but most couples don't match. I just couldn't believe all the hate for a guy who's the victim in all this—he's the one getting cheated on! Nobody deserves that, it doesn't matter how boring or ugly you are. It just seems like everybody is on the side of the guy who is screwing the wife! But I hear that guy is likeable, so I guess that goes a long way. That's why I used to tell my kids that kindness goes a long way, and this guy who is screwing Sofía, well he's getting used, but he's not a jerk; and the husband, well everybody thinks that kid is a jerk, but she's using him too. So, it's a case of two dummies getting used. Funny how life is, ain't it? So, who's the enemy? We all know who the enemy is. The enemy is in the mirror. Pretty deep shit, no? I read philosophy at night.

Hurricane Alice: What did Marissa tell Javi when she came to visit? If she's having sex with you, she's not having sex with the husband, so yes, I'm sure it's your baby. Wow, when I heard that, my mouth fell wide open and I just looked at Nick like—OH MY GOD! I can't, I can't, I tell you. And we know Marissa knows, because of course one of her kids don't look like the daddy. We don't tell Nick that, because we know that kid looks like her former Regional Supervisor Grant Welsh. Rumors, that's how they start. There is always some truth underneath.

Eric: Yep, that's what she told him. And we know she knows. Well, at least I know that Alice knows that she knows, but I don't care to know. It is what it is. Marissa probably did screw Grant Welsh. It was a similar situation as Javi, but it didn't last that long and I believe her. I think. But let me tell you, these women, I swear. How the rolls have changed.

Miguel: Trampolinas all of them, including Alice. I don't trust her as far as I can throw her, but you know what, we got a good thing and she is my baby's mama. I mean, I like Norton, he's a good guy. It doesn't matter to me. We're having fun and I love her and she loves me too and I love Norton. He's a great guy. But it is what it is like they say. Do I feel guilty about me continuing to screw my ex in front of such a nice guy as Norton? Just a little bit, but she's my baby's mama so I got dibs. So, I'm sure that's how it will eventually end up with Javi and Sofía as soon as he gets that damn DNA test.

Hurricane Alice's Mom: It's just all ridiculous; Sofía should just leave that little man and move in with her baby's father. I know he's poor or not rich or whatever, but I'm sure she can light a firecracker under his ass so he can get his act together. I mean she's beautiful, she can get any dummy to finish law school, I'm sure, with that adorable Latin face and her little body with that wet coochie that drives men crazy. Think about it, this little girl has these two fools doing whatever she wants. That's power. If you ask me who really runs the world, it's women. And of course, money, but man need money to get women so it's the ladies.

Hurricane Alice: You know what he said to me? I guess he feels bad; he said he only took the toothbrush because it was there in front of him. He was like, "I didn't fly over there to get DNA, I only went to see her and the baby." But he knew, since I threatened him with bodily harm that he would try, and he did—the huge balls on this guy stealing from a child. I actually didn't think he was going to really do it. I'm so proud. He needs to win the lottery or something. I keep telling him to lie to her and pretend that a rich uncle left him six figures or he's getting a book deal—he did write that little short film and she was impressed with that. These starving artists, I gotta tell you. But what can you do, Javi is a Suckerfish—from day one, first day he saw her, she had him in her little pocket. We call her the Black Widow; God help us if she ever found out. But she's Colombian; she's in that cartel, I'm sure. Her cousin told us she used to date a drug trafficker back there, and then Javi said the guy was also Palestinian so what do you know. I swear it's like a soap opera—the whole entire office; me with Miguel and Javi with Sofía, it's just so crazy. I can't, I can't … but we'll see what happens. As far as everyone knows, that's Javi's kid—DNA test or no DNA test. But he's a suckerfish, he loves her so much that even if the test comes out positive, he's not going to do anything about it. He says he will confront her, but he won't. He doesn't want to cause any drama, that's what he said. Oh well, things are going to change drastically for that suckerfish once he finds out that's his daughter—kids are so difficult. His head is going to explode because no matter what, that's your blood running around. That little baby is yours forever, bought and sold for life. I should have had cats instead.

Gray Cat, Purple Rug

On that rainy morning of that last day, I delivered some homemade *ajiaco*, Colombian chicken soup, to my mother and my ex-girlfriend, who was expecting a child that might be her husband's or mine.

I went to see my mother first. Her apartment was fifteen minutes away from me. We talked for a little bit. I was excited about the soup; it was a good batch, I told her. She wanted me to deposit a check for her. She didn't come out of the house much unless it was with me. I grabbed the check, kissed her on the forehead, and left.

I was pretending like I had work that day. If she knew I'd taken the day off, she would have pestered me about taking her shopping to Walmart or Macy's. Who wants to go shopping at Wal-Mart on their day off?

My ex-girlfriend's job was five minutes from my apartment. I parked and she was already outside, waiting for me under the building's parking garage, trying to avoid the light drizzle.

I walked through the rain and handed her the lunch bag.

"What happened to the umbrella?" she asked.

"That thing is bulky, I just wanted to get out the car fast,"

I said. "Here is the soup, cookies, bananas, and a couple of tangerines."

"Thank you," she said.

I visualized placing my right hand on her belly. She was three months. She kissed me on my wet cheek. She then reminded me of the weekend trip with her husband, and an upcoming overnight work trip with her boss the following week.

I acquiesced; we kissed again and I left.

I stayed up late the night before making her favorite soup, using all organic ingredients in case I was the father of the baby.

When I got home, I drank some coffee, put on some depressing music, and watched my gray cat be lazy on the purple rug.

I sent my ex a quick phone text about the limes in the lunch bag. Did I mention them?

She will see them.

Then I started texting an old love of mine, in another state, trying to convince her to come the following weekend, despite the world possibly ending soon, "We could have one last good weekend before nuclear annihilation … wink, wink."

She took too long to respond, and I got bored.

I went on Twitter and tweeted photos of my cat. I retweeted stories about the *ten items to include in your nuclear fallout emergency kit,* and *an easy pistachio cake recipe for busy professionals.*

I logged into my bank account:

$$-\$400.12$$

"AMERICA MINUS FOUR-HUNDRED DOLLARS
AND TWELVE CENTS AUGUST 10, 2017."

I heated some of my homemade soup and texted again my pregnant ex, "Came out good, huh?"

"Eating it now. It's so good."

Read two short stories about Chileans in Russia written by Roberto Bolaño from Chile.

I avoided the television on specific instructions from Ray Bradbury (my favorite writer).

I got a text informing me that a co-worker's elderly father passed away. I wept. He came to our office once and made us some delicious gumbo. He gave everyone handmade wooden crosses and birdhouses. I gave one to my mother. He talked to us about surviving the Pearl Harbor attack and then meeting his wife the very next day.

I called my mother and told her I loved her. She said she enjoyed the soup so much she was taking a nap. We hung up and I started thinking about the conversation we had last Sunday after grocery shopping.

We were talking about dreams. She always dreams about food before someone dies. So I asked her what she dreams of when someone is going to have a baby.

"Did you get someone pregnant? Am I going to be a grandmother?" I laughed it off nervously and tried to change the subject.

"Just curious," I said.

"Aha! Just curious … just curious … give me a break."